D1515862

Sunny

Richelle.

Nick

ELMO

LIZ

EMILY RODDA'S
RAVEN HILL MYSTERIES

CASE #4: DEEP SECRETS

**Be on the lookout for all of
Emily Rodda's Raven Hill Mysteries:**

EMILY RODDA'S
RAVEN HILL MYSTERIES

CASE #4: DEEP SECRETS

Emily Rodda and Robert Sexton

SCHOLASTIC INC.

New York   Toronto   London   Auckland   Sydney
Mexico City   New Delhi   Hong Kong   Buenos Aires

ISBN 0-439-78249-X

12 11 10 9 8 7 6 5 4 3 2   6 7 8 9 10 11/0

Printed in the U.S.A.
First American edition, March 2006

Contents

1

The letter

No matter how hard we try to organize part-time work for Help-for-Hire Inc., our gang's job agency, we always seem to miss out during school vacation times. And spring break was looking like yet another vacation where we'd have no money-earning work to do.

It was Thursday afternoon, and school had just ended.

The gang — Liz Free, Tom Moysten, Richelle Brinkley, Nick Kontellis, and Sunny Chan — was at my house, waiting for my dad to turn up and pay us.

I was there, too, of course. My name's Elmo Zimmer. Together, the six of us make up Help-for-Hire Inc.

On Thursday mornings before school, we deliver the *Pen* — the local paper — around Raven Hill. Dad owns the *Pen*, and he usually pays us as soon as we get back to the office. But this morning, he was out when we arrived.

We'd been wanting to have a meeting about the lack of work, but in fact, we hadn't talked too much about that. We'd started watching this game show on TV and gotten sucked in. Now we were keeping score to see who got the most points.

"We'd better find a job soon," said Tom gloomily. "Or we'll get stuck with cleaning up our rooms again."

"Shush!" ordered Richelle. "The last question's coming up."

She was really interested because she had a good chance of winning.

Tom, who's only good at questions about art and food, was last. Nick, who thinks he's the smartest, was running second last. Sunny was fourth, Liz was third, and Richelle and I were tied for the top score.

I was doing well because I read a lot and keep up with the news, due to my job at the *Pen*. Richelle was doing well because so many of the questions were about film stars, ads, and TV shows. She loves all that stuff.

We stopped talking and listened to the question. The host smiled widely, showing all his teeth, and talked at the same time.

"What is Saint Elmo's fire?" he said.

Everyone looked blank, then stared at me. I shrugged.

"Don't you know?" drawled Nick.

"No," I said. "I'm named Elmo because my grandad was named Elmo, and he named my dad Elmo. That's it."

The TV contestants didn't know, either. The buzzer sounded.

"Saint Elmo's fire," said the TV man, still smiling, "is a luminous glow sometimes seen around high, projecting objects such as ships' masts and church spires during thunderstorms, snowstorms, and dust storms. Saint Elmo is the patron saint of sailors, and Saint Elmo's fire is said to be a sign of his protection."

"I was just about to say that," said Tom.

Sure.

"I won!" beamed Richelle. "And Elmo," she added.

"Crazy trick questions," Nick sneered. You wouldn't call him a bad loser, exactly. You'd call him a terrible loser.

Just at that moment, Dad came in. He was holding a piece of paper.

"Elmo," he said. "Guess what I've got."

"Our money?" asked Tom hopefully.

Dad nodded absentmindedly. "Oh, yes," he said, as if it didn't matter at all. "But, Elmo, I just received a letter from your great-aunt Vivien."

"Yeah? What about?" I said. It might seem strange that I was interested in a letter from my grandfather's sister. But my great-aunt Vivien wasn't exactly a big letter writer.

"Aunt Vivien — I can't believe it," Dad was saying to the others. "For all I knew she was dead. She lives in this huge old house way out in the sticks. It must be the third letter in thirty years."

"Dad, what does she want?" I asked, for the second time.

"You might not believe this," Dad said with a laugh. "But she wants Help-for-Hire to come and work for her. For money. And all expenses paid."

"What?" Now I was really astounded. Great-aunt Vivien and my grandfather hadn't liked each other much. Grandad used to say his sister was certifiably nuts and unworthy of the Zimmer name. She'd severed all ties with our side of the family. I'd never even met her.

"You won't want to do it, of course —" Dad began. Then he broke off in surprise because the gang was cheering, drowning him out.

"Saved!" chortled Tom. "Money!"

"A big, luxurious house," sighed Richelle.

"A vacation in the country for free!" grinned Liz.

"It won't be much of a vacation if I know Aunt Vivien," said Dad grimly.

That quieted them down.

"Ah . . . what do you mean, exactly, Zim?" asked Nick cautiously.

Dad ran his fingers through his hair in that way he does when he's stressed out.

"Well, I don't want to alarm you," he said — though I could see that he did, really. "But from what I remember of the old girl she wouldn't know a hard day's work if she fell over it. She's spent her whole life just traveling around the world and having fun."

"What's so bad about that?" asked Richelle, bewildered.

Dad shrugged. "Nothing so bad, I suppose," he admitted. "But what I mean is that she's never done a thing for anyone else in her life. She's never worked. She's just spent money. Stayed in expensive hotels, bought expensive clothes, and enjoyed herself."

Richelle went on looking blank. As far as she was concerned, this way of life sounded perfect.

Dad gave up trying to explain and went straight to the point.

"I think she's probably just asking you because . . . well, because it suits her. She thinks she's getting you cheap."

"Everyone gets us cheap," muttered Nick bitterly. He's always complaining our rates are too low. But, as Liz always says, no one'd be able to hire us to do odd jobs if we charged too much. Most people around Raven Hill couldn't afford it.

We looked at each other.

"Well, what do you think?" I asked.

"I'd like to go," Liz said. "I'd love a few days out of the city."

Sunny nodded. "We can go for long walks in our free time," she said.

Richelle shuddered. That was the last thing she had on her mind. But . . .

"I'd like some time in a really lovely house," she said. "Those old country mansions can be fabulous."

"I could do some sketching. And think of the meals," Tom put in. "Big country breakfasts, morning snack time with biscuits and jam, enormous country lunches, afternoon snack time with chocolate-chip cookies and homemade lemonade. Dinners with . . ."

"I don't know," said Nick, breaking in before Tom actually started drooling. "Stuck way out there for days. Paid peanuts."

"We don't all have to go," said Liz in an offhand sort of way. "You could stay home, Nick. We'll just split the peanuts five ways instead of six."

Liz is smart. If you ever want to change Nick's mind, talk about money.

"Still . . . all expenses paid," he said thoughtfully. "It's probably worth it. I guess."

"So it's on?" asked Tom eagerly.

They hadn't asked me what I thought. They were just assuming I was in. After all, Vivien was *my* great-aunt. But I really didn't want to go.

"I don't know Aunt Vivien at all, you know," I told them. "And even Dad has only met her a few times. The job might be a complete disaster."

5

"We won't blame you, Elmo," said Liz. "And anyway, everything'll be fine."

"Sure. What can go wrong?" shrugged Tom.

That should have made us all stop and think. Anytime anyone's ever said that in the past, we've found ourselves up to our necks in trouble.

But no one said anything. The others were all too busy with their own private dreams about how good the new job was going to be. And I was too busy being nervous because Aunt Vivien was my aunt, and the job had come to us through Dad. Whatever they said, everyone would blame me if they didn't enjoy themselves.

"Dad, she did actually ask for the whole gang, didn't she?" I said. "I mean, how would she know Help-for-Hire even exists?"

"She's been reading about you in the *Pen*, apparently," Dad mumbled. "Following the stories about your crime-busting activities. Not that she's interested in that, of course. It's the job agency she's after."

I raised my eyebrows in surprise. "How would Aunt Vivien see the *Pen*?"

"The *Pen*'s sent to her every week," Dad said, looking a bit embarrassed. "I organized that after I took over the paper. After your grandfather died."

"I didn't know that!" I exclaimed.

"I thought — well, at the time I thought it might be nice to try to keep in touch," Dad muttered. "These family feuds are stupid. But she never wrote thanking me or anything. As far as I knew, she was throwing the papers straight into the trash. But I guess she wasn't."

"Of course she wasn't." Soft-hearted Liz beamed. "That's so nice. After all this time, the dear old lady wants to get to know Elmo. That's why she's asked us to work for her, for sure. It's all just an excuse to see him."

"She's never shown any interest before," said Dad doubtfully. "We sent her a photograph when he was a baby, but . . ."

"I bet she thought he was so cute and cuddly," Tom teased.

Richelle giggled, and I felt myself blushing.

"Anyway, that decides it for sure," Liz announced. "We'll definitely go."

The others nodded.

Dad ran his fingers through his hair again. "Well, it's your funeral," he sighed. "You'll have to check it out with your parents. Give us a call tonight, to confirm. Then I'll write to Vivien and set it up. You'll go by train. How about you plan to leave right after the next *Pen* delivery?"

"But that's a whole week away!" exclaimed Liz. "Can't we make it sooner?"

Dad shook his head. "Not really," he said. "It all has to be organized by letter. There's no phone or e-mail at Mistfall."

"Not even a *phone?*" squeaked Richelle in horror.

"Mistfall!" breathed Liz at the same moment. "What a great name."

"What's great about it? It sounds sort of . . . damp," quavered Richelle. She touched her long, wavy fair hair in a worried sort of way. A damp place with no phone! Richelle was starting to wish she hadn't agreed to this job so easily.

And I was wishing I hadn't agreed at all.

2

Destination: nowhere

Dad wrote to Aunt Vivien the next day, and the reply came back early the following week. Aunt Vivien was looking forward to seeing us, especially me. She'd expect us to arrive by train on Friday.

There was no discussion about which train. It turned out there was only one. And there wasn't any discussion about how long we'd stay, either. There was no train back to the city from Kneebone, Aunt Vivien said, till Monday morning.

"*Kneebone?*" snorted Nick, when he heard this. "I don't *believe* there's a place called Kneebone!"

"There is," I said. "Aunt Vivien's address is 'Mistfall via Kneebone.' I saw it on her letter."

"Well, whoever heard of a train station where the trains only stop twice a week!" exclaimed Richelle.

I shrugged. "Want to change your minds?" I asked hopefully.

"No!" said Liz. "We're going to have our vacation in the country, and you're going to have that reunion with your great-aunt if it kills me, Elmo Zimmer."

"It might," I said darkly.

"Mistfall via Kneebone," murmured Tom. "Sounds like a good place to die."

He thought he was joking.

✿

On Friday morning, we were on our way. We'd already changed trains once, and we still had hours of travel stretching in front of us. No one was in a particularly good mood.

"I was thinking, you know," Liz said, staring out the window. "Aunt Vivien will have to send two cars to pick us up. Otherwise, we won't all fit in."

"It'll probably be a cattle truck," said Tom drearily.

"Sure, sure." Nick jeered. "They'll send a car for us and a cattle truck for you, Moysten."

"At least I'll be in better company than I'm in now."

"Can't you two ever stop?" cried Liz.

I didn't say anything. I was too busy thinking. I wasn't looking forward to seeing Aunt Vivien.

Grandad hadn't liked her. He'd always said she was certifiably nuts, as he put it. I imagined some embarrassing, vain, fussy old woman wearing fancy clothes who laughed all the time. She'd probably bore everyone silly with stories about her travels. She'd probably want to kiss me and leave red lipstick all over my face.

Richelle was sulking. It had started because Nick had promised to bring his cell phone with him, and then at the last minute had left it at home.

"I couldn't help it, Richelle," he'd told her. "It's not working properly. It's got to be fixed."

"You should have checked it out last week!" she'd pouted. "Now we're going to be stuck out in the middle of nowhere without a phone."

"Come on, Richelle," Liz said. "Even *you* can live without a phone for a couple of days."

"Yeah," said Tom. "It'll give your ear a chance to get back to normal."

Her eyes widened. "What do you mean?"

"Oh, you know," he said casually. "The way your right ear's sort of flattened out and gotten bigger than the other one? That's because of the phone, isn't it?"

Richelle's hand flew to her right ear, and she turned crimson.

Tom turned to Nick. "You've noticed Richelle's ear, haven't you, Nick?"

Nick nodded seriously. "Oh, yeah," he said. "But I didn't want to say anything."

By now, Richelle had one hand on her ear, and one over her mouth, and her eyes looked as though they were going to fall out of her head.

"Richelle, it's all right," said Liz, half-laughing, half-angry with Tom and Nick.

"There's nothing wrong with your ear, Richelle," sighed Sunny. "They're just playing around."

But it took a while for Richelle to calm down. And when she finally did, she went into a long, injured silence that lasted for practically the whole trip.

❁

By the time another hour had passed, Nick, Liz, Richelle, and Tom were asleep, rocking with the movement of the train. Sunny was still awake, but she was just staring out the window as if she was hypnotized.

There was practically no one left in our car except these two big, mean-looking guys wearing dark suits and sunglasses. They kept looking at us, and grinning at one another, as though there was something about us they found funny.

They worried me.

I wondered where they were going. As far as I could tell, they were going nowhere. The same as us.

Destination: Kneebone. Code name for nowhere. A tiny dot on the map with a whole lot of space around it. One of lots of other tiny dots, linked only by the train line and the road that ran alongside it.

Maybe the men were going to another one of the dots. To rob a bank, maybe. Or to set up shop as funeral directors. Or they could be railway detectives who rode the train all day and night, looking for people who hadn't paid their fares, or put their feet on the seats.

Anyway, I wished they'd move into another car. But even if they did, they wouldn't be very far away. There were only two cars for people in the whole train. The rest of the train was made up of freight cars.

I looked out the window and wished I'd come down with chicken pox or tonsilitis. Even an earache. Anything to get out of this.

But there was no way out. To Kneebone we were going, whether I liked it or not. So I decided to get out of the situation the only way I could. I closed my eyes like the others, and dozed.

I woke up when the train pulled into this tiny little station. "Kneebone!" called the guard, walking through the carriage and roaring as though it was full of people. "Kneebone!"

We gathered up our stuff and climbed out of the train. Flies descended on us happily.

"Good luck!" the guard said, and winked at me.

Then he stood back.

The two men in suits were getting out, too.

There was no one to meet us. Not that we could see, anyway.

We stood around on the station platform for a while, just waiting. But still no one appeared on the road outside. No minibus. No fleet of cars. No cattle truck.

Tom found a small poster lying on the platform. It was advertising a wrestling match. Here in the Kneebone Town Hall on Saturday night.

"Who says this place isn't jumping?" he grinned.

One of the wrestlers was wearing a Roman gladiator's costume. He even had a wreath of leaves around his head. He was called "The Killer." The other was more like the evil monster in a late-night movie. He was "The Freak." They were both wearing face paint, and were glaring at one another, with clenched fists.

Tom got out his pen and, in his words, gave the wrestlers "a bit of life."

He gave them bow ties, earrings, nose rings, little curved horns, striped socks, and flower tattoos on their chests.

"How's that?" he said, when he'd finished.

"Much better," said Liz. But I noticed that she glanced up the tiny platform and back again in a worried sort of way. She was wondering what we were going to do if no one turned up for us.

Richelle didn't care about worrying anyone.

"Nick Kontellis," she said sternly. "If you'd only said your cell phone wasn't working, I finally could have convinced my dad to get me one. Now look at the mess we're in. We can't even call a taxi."

"A taxi?" Nick snorted. "Where do you think you are, Richelle? There are no taxis here."

I left Richelle and Nick arguing about the phone we didn't have, and went to find someone who could help us.

There was a sort of shed in the center of the platform. I knocked at the door.

After a while, a man came out and stared at me. He was an old guy who needed a shave and a set of teeth. He had on a railroad hat and coat so I guessed he worked there.

"Excuse me," I said. "Somebody was coming to meet us."

"I haven't seen no one," he said.

"Someone from Mistfall." I thought the name might mean something to him. I pointed in the direction I thought the cars or whatever might come from. "It's that way, isn't it?"

He pushed his cap back on his head. A few bits of white hair poked out from under the peak.

"Mistfall? Now lemme see . . ."

I could tell he'd take all day to think about it.

"It's okay. Thanks, anyway." I nodded for the gang to follow me and headed for the exit.

"Mistfall," the old man called out behind us. "Yeah. Mistfall's about six miles up the road. Dunno why you wanna go there."

"My great-aunt lives there," I said.

"That right?" he said. He munched his bare gums together.

We didn't want to stand there talking to the guy so we kept moving. Out of the station, onto the road.

The guys in suits had disappeared. I wondered where they'd gone.

The road was just a dirt track. And Kneebone itself seemed to consist entirely of a general store, a gas station, a tiny fire station, a diner, three houses, and a rickety wooden building with a corrugated iron roof and TOWN HALL painted over its door.

My heart leaped as I saw a cloud of dust heading down the road toward us.

"There you are," said Liz brightly. "Our ride."

We picked up our bags and waited.

3

Death Valley

The dustball turned into a big, black car with darkened windows. It swung off the road and stopped, just in front of us. We started walking toward it.

Then, suddenly, the two big guys in suits wandered out of the diner. Casually, they crossed the road, threw their bags into the car, and got into the backseat.

I couldn't see the driver. Nor could I see the men once they were inside. I could see only our grotesque reflections in the one-way glass. We all had big heads, very big noses, and tiny little bodies.

And very depressed expressions.

The car roared away, leaving us standing in a cloud of dust.

"Buses usually meet the trains at country stations," Tom said, after a moment. "So we'll just wait here till a bus comes, okay?"

"Dream on, Moysten," Nick drawled. "There's not going to be a bus."

"There are always buses in the country," Tom said. "Eventually. I know these things, Kontellis."

The toothless railroad guy toddled up to us.

"No good standin' there," he said.

"We're waiting for a bus," said Tom politely.

The man laughed, showing all his gums. "Be a long wait," he said. "Isn't due till Monday morning."

"Thanks," Nick said. He glared at Tom, then looked around scornfully. "What a place!" he hissed.

"Nothing wrong with this place. City kids. Got no sense, have ya?" the toothless guy mumbled as he turned away.

Nick was in his worst aggro mood. He followed the old man.

"What do you mean by that?"

"Just what I said. Shoulda found out where you was going before ya left home, shouldn't ya?"

Liz stepped between them. "I'm sorry," she said. "It's just that we've come all this way, and we're a bit tired."

"Well, little lady, you're gonna be a lot more tired, time you get to Mistfall," croaked the toothless man.

Liz tried to smile. "How far is it?" she asked.

"Six miles, about," said the man, with a satisfied smile. "That way." He pointed to the left, down a dirt road that stretched off into the distance like Death Valley.

"OK," Liz said, firmly leading Nick away. "Thank you. We'd better get started, then."

Oh, no, I thought. *Oh, please, let me still be dreaming.*

But I wasn't dreaming. I was in Kneebone. And so was everyone else. This was hideous reality.

"Look at yer," the old man called after us as we trailed away. "Half of yer's not dressed for a six-mile hike."

I glanced back at him. He grinned widely and pointed at Richelle. "By the look of them shoes, you'll be carrying her before you get half way," he yelled.

With a cackle of laughter, he went back to the station.

And we started walking.

Six hot, dusty, deadly miles to Mistfall.

"What's six miles in city blocks?" Richelle asked.

"Dozens," said Sunny, who was already on her way. "Come on, guys, or we'll never get there."

Richelle looked as if she was going to die. She swatted helplessly at some flies.

"Come on!" Sunny called as she jogged on the spot about fifty feet up the road. "Six miles is nothing."

But we'd only been walking ten minutes before I'd decided that anything would be better than this. It would be nice to be home, digging the moldy vegetables out of the fridge crisper. It would be heavenly to be scraping the congealed fat out of the backyard grill.

My bag was getting heavier by the second. Richelle screamed every time a fly settled on her face. She made me edgy.

My sneakers had gotten thin underneath. I could feel every stone I walked on. I should have accepted the offer of a new pair when Dad was feeling generous a couple of weeks ago. But my old ones felt so comfortable and lived-in then. Now I might as well have taken them off for all the good they were doing.

Nick made up his mind the walk wasn't going to beat him. He strode ahead with Sunny and Liz, leaving Tom, Richelle, and me behind.

As we trudged along, a few cars and a pickup truck passed by. A couple of the drivers stared at us. But no one stopped.

"I thought people were supposed to be friendly in the country," complained Richelle.

"We'd be stupid to take a ride from a stranger, anyway," said Liz. "You can get killed that way."

"I'm practically dead now," sniffed Richelle.

A shiny green SUV roared by. We were covered in its dust and had to stop, coughing and spluttering.

But do you think the driver cared? No way. He sat there, hiding behind his sunglasses, pretending not to see us. His ponytail was flying in the wind as he roared past. He had the radio blaring. He looked as if he didn't have a worry in the world. And he was drinking a can of Coke.

We would have killed for that can of Coke.

"Can you *believe* he could do that?" Richelle screeched.

But in spite of him, and Richelle's screams, and the stones, we finally reached a little intersection where a faded sign said MISTFALL 2 MILES. Liz, Sunny, and Nick were sitting on a rock waiting for us.

"Richelle," Sunny called. "See? You did it. Just shows what you can do if you try."

Richelle stared at her but said nothing. That was worse than if she'd shouted at the top of her voice.

Just then, a cloud of dust appeared over the brow of a hill ahead of us. We all stood back as the car passed. We didn't want another dust bath.

It was the same black monster that had picked up the guys

in the suits. But it seemed to be empty of passengers now. It had dropped off the guys and was heading back to base.

It wasn't any help. But at least it gave us something to talk about, besides our sore feet and the flies.

"Who do you think those guys were?" Sunny asked.

"Probably a couple of spies," Nick said.

"Don't be stupid, Nick," Richelle said. "There's nothing out here to spy on."

Liz sighed. "Whoever they are, and whatever they're doing, I'll bet they're having a better time than us."

And no one was arguing with her about that.

4

Mistfall

As we got closer to Mistfall, Sunny ran on ahead of us — up a hill and over the other side. A few minutes later, she came jogging back.

"I wish she'd stop doing that," groaned Tom. "It makes me even more exhausted just looking at her."

"Hey, guys," Sunny shouted. "It's just over the hill. You can see it. Just a few more minutes. Come on!"

On the train I'd been dreading seeing Aunt Vivien. But now, after walking through Death Valley for what seemed like six thousand miles instead of six, I couldn't wait.

Everyone else must have felt the same way. They all started walking faster. Even Richelle.

We talked about what we were going to do when we arrived.

Richelle wanted a long, hot shower. All Nick and Liz cared about was a long, cool drink. Tom wanted food. Lots of food. I wanted two new feet. Sunny probably wanted to go back to the railroad station and start running all over again.

Full of new energy, we powered up that hill. And just as Sunny had promised, we were soon stumbling down the other side, with our eyes fixed on the big house in the valley.

It wasn't exactly what anyone had expected.

"Oh, what a marvelous old place," said Liz. But she didn't sound as enthusiastic as usual.

We slowed down a bit, staring at what was going to be our home for the next couple of days.

One thing was for sure. It was a big house. A very big house. It was made of big blocks of gray stone.

One end of the building looked a bit like one of those forts you see in films about Europe in the Middle Ages. It had a tower with slitted windows. You could just imagine archers shooting at the enemy from there. The other end of the house was like a church with a tall steeple.

Sticking up from the tower and the steeple were long thin lightning rods.

"It looks half like a castle and half like a pretend church," said Richelle. "It's weird."

"It's a monstrosity," said Nick. "Who'd build a house like that?"

"Dr. Frankenstein," Tom said.

"And you." Richelle snapped at him. "You like all that weirdo stuff."

"Yeah," Tom grinned, feasting his eyes on the weird old place. "Look at the turrets and spires and stuff. And the stained-glass windows. Isn't it great?"

Nick sneered.

We finally reached the gate at the bottom of the hill. It was high, with iron railings. MISTFALL was engraved on a dull brass plate screwed on to one side. We stood looking up the weedy drive. The door was at the tower end of the house, and so huge that three of us could have walked through it side by side.

The garden was completely overgrown — just a mass of huge, spreading bushes and long grass, with lots of flowers growing wild everywhere, and bunches of seed pods rattling in the breeze. It reminded me of an old cemetery, except that the gravestones were missing.

The whole place was definitely weird, and very spooky-looking. And it was the middle of the day.

I could imagine it in the full moon, with long shadows making the whole scene even more scary. Like houses they have in movies where you've got witches and vampires and rats and blood dripping from the ceiling.

We backed away from the gate.

"This place gives me the creeps," Richelle whispered.

"Why are you whispering?" Tom whispered.

"Oh, come on," Liz said loudly. "Let's go in."

"Yes," said Sunny, putting her hand through the big iron gate railings. "We won't do any good standing here."

The gate creaked open. Little bits of rusty iron fell off it as it swung back, away from us.

"Well, we made it," I said, trying to sound cheerful.

No one answered me as we walked quickly up the drive.

There was a big, white Rolls Royce car parked in a garage behind the house. The garage doors were open, and we could see it clearly, just sitting there.

"We could have all fit into that," said Richelle crossly. "And I've always wanted to ride in a Rolls."

No one answered her, either.

We'd almost reached the house when the big front door swung open. A frowning, black-haired, thin-lipped woman emerged from the dimness and stood staring at us.

I opened my mouth to say something, but the words died in my throat as she abruptly turned back into the house and spoke to someone standing behind her. The next moment a bony-faced man with a thin black mustache appeared beside her.

Who's that? I thought, confused. Dad said Aunt Vivien wasn't married.

"Hey, you kids! Clear off!" the man shouted.

We stopped dead. Everyone looked at me. I could feel my face getting red. I shuffled forward a couple of steps.

"It's me, Aunt Vivien," I said to the woman, trying to smile. "Elmo."

The woman gaped at me. "*Who?*" she demanded.

My stomach was tying itself into knots. This was terrible! Could Aunt Vivien possibly have forgotten about inviting us? And why didn't she recognize me? She'd seen my picture in the *Pen*.

I cleared my throat. "You know," I said. "Elmo. Your nephew. Your . . . um . . . grand-nephew. Come for the weekend. To work. Dad wrote to you. Remember?"

A strange expression crossed the woman's face. She seemed to be thinking quickly. Then she bared her teeth in what was probably supposed to be a smile.

"Oh. Yes. It had slipped my mind you were coming today,"

she said. "But I'm afraid it's not very convenient. Maybe another weekend. You'd better run along home now."

She started to close the door.

I heard the gang groaning softly behind me.

"But-but, Aunt Vivien, it was all organized. You wrote to Dad —" I shouted in desperation. "He wrote back to you. He told you we were coming. And we can't go home. There's no train."

The woman hesitated. She muttered something I couldn't hear to the man beside her. He shook his head and muttered back, as if he was arguing with her. But finally she opened the door wide again and beckoned impatiently.

"You'd better come in, then," she snapped.

We stumbled up the steps. Not that I wanted to. And I'm sure the rest of the gang was feeling exactly like I was. But at that moment we didn't have any choice.

The woman watched us silently as we crowded inside. Now that I was closer to her, I could see that she was much younger than she'd seemed at a distance. And very much younger than Aunt Vivien could possibly be.

My surprise must have shown in my face, because again she gave that awful, fake smile. Her thin lips were covered with very dark red lipstick, and her eyebrows were as thin as pencil lines.

"What a mix-up," she murmured. "I can't imagine what you'll think of us."

"You're not my Aunt Vivien, are you?" I blurted out.

She raised her eyebrows. "Of course I'm not, dear," she said. "I'm Miss Zimmer's housekeeper, Mrs. Everedd. And this is my husband, who manages the farm." She gestured at the bony-faced man hovering behind her. He nodded briefly at me, uncomfortably fingering his thin mustache.

"Oh . . . er . . . I'm . . . er . . . sorry. It's just I haven't seen my great-aunt since . . . um . . . well, I've never met her, actually," I heard myself burbling.

I knew I was sounding like a complete idiot. I was so embarrassed I felt as though I was melting.

"That's quite all right," smiled the woman. "I understand. Unfortunately, Miss Zimmer hadn't told me you were expected. She's a bit forgetful these days. But never mind."

Great. No wonder we hadn't been met at the station. Aunt Vivien had completely forgotten we were even coming. I remembered Grandad's unflattering description of her. She must have gotten worse with age. What had I gotten the gang into?

"Where is she?" I asked, looking around.

For the first time, I noticed just how nice the house was inside. It was beautiful, really, with polished wood and thick rugs on the floor, and a clean, fresh smell. Not at all what you would have expected.

"Miss Zimmer hasn't been very well today. She's resting," the housekeeper said smoothly. "Why don't you go visit the kitchen and have something to eat? My husband will look after you. I'll go and see if Miss Zimmer's awake."

"Thank you, Mrs. . . . ?" I hesitated. I'd completely forgotten her name.

"Mrs. Everedd," she said. And again she smiled. A smile that was more like a snarl than anything else.

"Mrs. Never-dead, more like it," Tom breathed in my ear.

I smothered a hysterical snort of laughter. Mr. and Mrs. Never-dead. That would be right. As we followed the silent man to the kitchen, I decided that the Never-deads were the perfect ending to a perfect nightmare.

Little did I know that it was just the beginning.

5

Hello, Aunt Vivien

The kitchen was huge and bright, and paneled with honey-colored wood. There was a long table and a dresser stacked with colorful plates at one end.

The table stood in front of a big, wide window — nothing like the narrow windows you could see from the road. It faced out to the hillside behind the house.

The view was lovely. The hill was green and covered with trees. All sorts of birds flew around, and there were deer grazing in groups.

"Look at that!" breathed Liz, gazing out at the view with a dreamy look on her face.

"Look at *that!*" muttered Tom. He pointed. His eyes were bulging. Mr. Never-dead had opened a door to reveal a giant walk-in pantry stacked with food, and two tall fridges.

"Sit down," Mr. Never-dead called over his shoulder, foraging in the pantry.

We did. Suddenly, we were feeling a lot better. Cake, we were all picturing. Apple pie. Hot scones. Cold lemonade.

But, in the end, the man came out carrying a small packet of plain crackers, and a half-used bottle of orange soda. He put them on the table, then, sighing, went off to get glasses and a jug of water from the tap.

"Dig in," he said, slamming the glasses down.

He leaned against one of the cupboards and watched us.

We sat there nibbling crackers and pouring soda. We were all hungry and thirsty, and so we were grateful, in a way, for anything we got. But it was a bit of a letdown after all our greedy imaginings.

We were still sitting there about fifteen minutes later. We'd finished the crackers and the soda, but there didn't seem much point in moving. Then the sound of two pairs of footsteps in the next room made us all turn our heads.

"They're in here, Miss Zimmer," we heard Mrs. Never-dead saying.

The next moment, they were in the kitchen. Mrs. Never-dead was holding Aunt Vivien tightly by the arm. I decided the old lady must be frailer than I'd thought.

"Well, here they are," Mrs. Never-dead said loudly. She pointed to me. "There's Elmo, see?"

My first sight of Aunt Vivien gave me quite a shock. I hadn't expected her to be young, or very good-looking, or anything. But I hadn't expected her to be like she was, either.

She wasn't as wrinkled as I'd thought she'd be, but she was twice as ugly. I have to say that because it's true. She'd put on a lot of makeup to try to brighten herself up, but it didn't help. If anything, it made things worse. Her straight, stringy hair hung to her shoulders. She would have been tall if she hadn't stooped so much. But she did stoop.

And her clothes! They were incredibly depressing. I don't care much about clothes myself, but you didn't have to be Richelle to think Aunt Vivien was in a pretty bad state.

She wore a grungy skirt that went up and down at the hem, a checkered blouse, a ragged-looking cardigan, and a string of beads that fit so tightly around her neck that they looked like they were choking her.

She was also wearing thick woolen tights and sneakers. Very worn sneakers. Worse than mine!

But it wasn't just her face and clothes that startled me. It was the way she was.

I'd expected someone who was talkative, and confident — even if she *was* certifiably nuts. But in fact my aunt was the opposite. She seemed very, very nervous. Her eyes darted everywhere as Mrs. Never-dead led her forward. She sniffed, and dabbed at her nose with a crumpled tissue. And she didn't say a word — to me, or anyone else.

"It seems there's been a mistake, Elmo," said Mrs. Never-dead. "When Miss Zimmer got your father's letter, she thought he wrote 'next month,' not 'next week.' She wouldn't have agreed to the visit now — not in her present state of health."

"Oh, yes," Richelle said eagerly. "That's an easy mistake to make. We'll just go straight home." Her eyes sparkled at the thought of getting away.

"Miss Zimmer was going to suggest the same thing," said Mrs. Never-dead. She turned to Aunt Vivien. "Weren't you,

Miss Zimmer?" she asked loudly. And I could have sworn her hand tightened on the old woman's arm.

Aunt Vivien nodded and mumbled.

"First thing in the morning," said Mrs. Never-dead. "Seeing as you said there were no more trains today."

"There are no trains till Monday!" Liz exclaimed.

Mrs. Never-dead's face fell. Aunt Vivien sniffed uncomfortably, and dabbed her nose again.

"That's okay," Richelle said with her most winning smile. "I was thinking. We don't want to be any trouble by staying till Monday. Maybe Mr. Never — um, I mean, Mr. Everedd — could drive us. I saw a Rolls in the garage. We'd all fit into that."

Mrs. Never-dead glanced at her husband, and frowned. "Unfortunately, that's impossible," she snapped. "The Rolls needs repair. It can't be driven. There's no way in the world we can take you to the city."

You could see that she was telling the truth. She'd have loved to get rid of us. She hesitated. Just for a moment, she seemed at a loss as to what to do next.

I took the opportunity to speak to Aunt Vivien directly. I'm usually quite shy, but she seemed even more nervous than I was. And I found myself feeling quite worried about her.

"It's nice to meet you after all this time, Aunt Vivien," I said. "These are the other members of Help-for-Hire."

She sniffed anxiously. Her eyes widened.

"Sunny, Liz, Nick, Tom, and Richelle," I told her, speaking slowly and pointing at the gang one at a time. "You remember. You saw their pictures in the *Pen*, didn't you?"

She swallowed, nodded, and glanced nervously at Mrs. Never-dead. "Yes," she whispered.

"I think Miss Zimmer is getting overtired," said Mrs. Never-dead, raising her thin black eyebrows. She began ushering Aunt Vivien out of the room.

As she went, she looked back over her shoulder at her husband. "Take them out to the yard," she snapped at him. "They can clean it up. Later, they can clean out the Rolls garage. And the well."

He cleared his throat, as though he was going to argue with her again.

"They should be outside," she said firmly. "In the open air. Miss Zimmer tells me they're here to work. So they can work. The yard should keep them busy for a while."

She gave Aunt Vivien a little push, and propelled her out of sight.

Mr. Never-dead took us outside to clean up the yard. He handed us each a plastic bag.

"Pick up every scrap of paper you can see," he said.

So we started picking up papers. It was just like being on detention.

This was turning out to be the worst day of my life. And the others were griping about everything, which didn't help.

Tom kept complaining that he was still hungry.

Richelle and Nick — superior, never-get-anything-wrong Nick — were whispering about Aunt Vivien's clothes.

Liz and Sunny were embarrassed for me, because my aunt was so weird.

But I was puzzled and worried. Aunt Vivien might not be the cleverest and most beautiful woman in the world, but she was still my aunt. And I couldn't help remembering how nervous she'd seemed. And how tightly Mrs. Never-dead had gripped her arm.

There was something very strange going on.

6

Settling in

In spite of all our complaints, we stuck to the job. It was boring work, but it wasn't as if it was too difficult. And looking for garbage gave us a chance to see what the grounds around the house were like.

There were two garages. One for the Rolls, and a locked one, which Mr. Never-dead said was being used as a storeroom.

The Rolls garage looked as if it had been used as a storeroom, too. On every wall there were shelves from floor to ceiling stacked with boxes and papers and other junk.

There was a shed with a noisy generator in it chugging away making electricity for the house. Aunt Vivien had to make her own power.

Luckily, though, she was obviously connected to town water. The well hadn't been used for years.

Because, eventually, we found it, too. It was quite a long way from the house, in a sort of gully. It was just a very deep hole in the ground. There was no built-up wall around it like in pictures of Jack-and-Jill wells.

A heavy wooden lid was fitted over the top, to stop people

falling down by accident, we guessed. We moved the lid and dropped a stone down. It took a count of two before we heard it hit something that sounded tinny on the bottom.

"There's no water in it," exclaimed Sunny, in surprise.

"That's probably because it's clogged up with junk," I said.

"It's pretty deep," muttered Nick. "I'm not going down there."

"Me, neither," chorused Tom and Richelle.

Maybe we won't have to," said Liz hopefully. "Maybe it'll take us too long to do the other things. After all, we've only got today, and Saturday, and Sunday. . . ."

Her voice trailed off, and we all looked at each other. It sounded like an eternity.

In silence, we heaved the lid back onto the well, and went back to cleaning up.

○

When we thought we'd finished, we took the bags of paper to the back door and called out to Mrs. Never-dead.

"Good," she said, peering at us. "Now, get your bags. I'll show you your rooms and get you settled in."

"Oh, yes!" said Richelle, who'd been talking about having a shower ever since we got there.

"You'll be sleeping in the west wing," she said. "This way."

We grabbed our bags and followed her out of the kitchen along a passage to a big room. The room was roughly round, like the spire. There was a huge table in the middle with twelve chairs around it.

On one side of the room, there was a big, heavy door. The carved panels gleamed, the brass doorknob shone. I wondered where the door led to, and asked Mrs. Never-dead.

"The tower wing," she said. "That whole area is Miss Zimmer's private quarters. Nothing to do with you."

Stairs curved up from the other end of the room to an open level — a "mezzanine," Mrs. Never-dead called it. She led us up, walking stiffly.

You could look down from the mezzanine and see everything in the room below. Lots of doors led off it. And there were more stairs going up above us to another level. I imagined there would be more rooms up there.

"Girls on this level," Mrs. Never-dead said crisply. "Boys on the next one up."

She opened one of the doors, and we looked inside.

"What a nice room," Liz smiled.

The bedroom was narrow near the door and widened out at the outside wall. It was like a big slice of cake with the point cut off.

The other bedrooms were the same. I was thankful to see that they were very clean. There was no dust at all, and a faint smell of furniture polish. The beds were already made up with crisp sheets.

I was thankful, but it was odd. There hadn't been time for Mrs. Never-dead to prepare all these bedrooms. They must have been made up before.

That meant Aunt Vivien really *had* been expecting us. *She must just be really forgetful*, I thought.

Mrs. Never-dead hadn't stopped talking.

"You girls use the bathroom along there," she said, pointing. "There's another one for the boys on their floor."

So, at last, we all had hot showers and changed into clean clothes.

"Aaaah," said Richelle, when we met downstairs later. "Now I feel human again. Even if I did get hurried out of the shower." She glared at Sunny, who just grinned and shrugged.

It was still daylight. We'd thought we might go for a walk and see the deer. But Mrs. Never-dead told us it was time for dinner.

We sat around the kitchen table and ate. I think I can honestly say it was the worst meal I've ever eaten. Worse than summer camp. And that's saying something.

We picked at the food. A few fatty, warmed-up meat bits cut from the very last remains of a roast; soggy, gray-green, half-cold brussels sprouts; lumpy mashed potatoes with brown bits in them; and gravy that tasted like mud.

Even Tom wouldn't eat it.

"Two stars," said Nick, judging it like a hotel. "Great beds, hopeless food."

Liz glanced at me, worried that I'd be hurt because this was my aunt's house. But I wasn't, really. Aunt Vivien wasn't responsible for this. It was all Mrs. Never-dead. She didn't want us here. And she was going all out to make sure we didn't want to be here, either.

Just then, the woman herself came back into the kitchen.

"All right," she said, looking at our plates. "Obviously, you weren't very hungry. You'd better clean up, then."

"I've got room for dessert," said Tom hopefully.

"There's no dessert, I'm afraid," snapped Mrs. Never-dead. "You can stack the dishwasher now, and then you'd better go straight to bed. You've got a hard day ahead of you tomorrow."

"But it's so early!" Richelle protested.

"We all go to bed early here, dear." The woman smiled thinly.

"I'd like to say good night to Aunt Vivien," I said.

"Oh, she's in bed," said Mrs. Never-dead. "She won't feel like seeing anyone now."

And obviously, as far as she was concerned, that was the end of it.

7

Lights out

I was changing, getting ready for bed, listening to the rumbling of distant thunder, when everything went black. I rushed out of my room and found myself staring at Nick and Tom, who'd done exactly the same. From the floor below we could hear Richelle complaining and calling out to Liz.

"Must be a blackout," said Nick. "It's thundering."

"Wake up, Kontellis. This house doesn't have the power on, so there can't be a blackout," jeered Tom. "They've just turned off the generator."

Richelle's voice rose to a shriek. "Nothing works!" she squealed. "My room's pitch-black!"

"Sorry about that," Mrs. Never-dead's voice echoed from downstairs. "We've turned off the generator. The power won't be back on till six in the morning."

"I can't see anything!" complained Richelle.

"Just go to sleep!" yelled Mrs. Never-dead.

"Might as well," Nick grumbled. "Nothing else to do." But there was no way I could sleep. I lay there in the dark, wide awake, listening to the thunder and the old house creaking.

After about half an hour, I'd had enough. I got up and pulled on my jeans.

I crept out into the hallway and knocked softly on Tom's door. He was in the room next to mine.

"It's Elmo," I whispered. "Are you awake?"

"No. Are you?" he whispered back. There was a thud as his feet hit the floor, then his door opened and he came out. His hair was sticking up on end, but he was fully dressed except for his shoes.

"This place spooks me," he said. "And I'm starving to death. I've been just lying there listening to my stomach rumble in time with the thunder."

Nick must have heard our voices. He came out of his room as well. He hadn't changed for bed, either. But his hair was as smooth as ever. I've never understood how Nick stays so neat.

"I think we should talk," I said in a low voice. "I think something's going on around here."

We crept down to the girls' level. We could hear low voices coming from Liz's room. We knocked and went in.

Richelle, Liz, and Sunny were sitting on the bed, just shadows in the dark.

"Can't you sleep, either?" Liz asked us.

"What do you think?" Nick grunted. "Who could sleep in this creepy house?"

"No offense, Elmo," said Sunny. "But he's right."

"Listen," I said. "I agree with you. But I don't think it's Aunt Vivien's fault."

So then we all started talking. And the more we talked, the more fishy the whole thing seemed.

On the one hand, we were told Aunt Vivien had forgotten we were coming. On the other hand, the beds were all made, and the pantry was stacked with food.

On the one hand, Aunt Vivien did appear to be sick. On the other hand, she'd been wanting to meet me. She'd said so in her letters. So you'd think that she'd be trying to talk to me, however sick she felt.

"It's really strange," whispered Liz. "It's as if —"

Then, suddenly, there was a crash and a bloodcurdling yell. We all leaped up as if we'd been shot.

"What was that?" whimpered Richelle.

"Someone's fallen over or something," suggested Liz.

We rushed out of the bedroom and felt our way down the stairs from the mezzanine, to the room with the big round table.

Now we could hear movement, and long, low groans. Somewhere in the house, someone was in pain.

Nick stopped, and listened. "It's coming from in there," he said, pointing at the heavy carved door that led to the tower wing.

"It must be Aunt Vivien," I exclaimed.

I skirted the table and fumbled my way to the door. I felt for the handle, turned it, shook it. It was locked.

Suddenly, I had a terrible feeling. I banged on the door. "Aunt Vivien!" I yelled. "Are you all right?"

"Elmo!" warned Liz. "Not so loud."

Outside there was a flash of lightning, and a huge clap of thunder.

And at that same moment, the heavy door clicked, as a key was turned in its lock. It swung open with a hideous creak.

Mrs. Never-dead was standing there, with a flashlight in her hand.

I heard Richelle give a squeal of fright. The woman was frowning with anger. She shone the flashlight in my face.

"What are you doing out of bed?" she asked sternly.

I don't know why we should have been scared of her. After all, we were in my aunt's house. And Mrs. Never-dead was only the housekeeper. But we *were* scared of her.

"We . . . heard someone screaming," I quavered, blinking in the light.

"Well, it's no concern of yours. Miss Zimmer had a bad nightmare. But she's all right now. There's nothing to worry about. Go back to bed."

What else could we do? She stood watching us as we trailed back up the stairs to the mezzanine. Then she slammed the door, and we heard the lock click again as the key was turned.

"I think we should go back to bed, like she says," whispered Nick. "Everything seems quiet now."

"I want to see if Aunt Vivien's all right!" I said fiercely.

Liz patted my arm. "It probably was just a nightmare, Elmo," she said.

"And think about it," Sunny added. "We don't know this house, and we haven't got a flashlight. You'll just have to wait till morning, and talk to Aunt Vivien then."

What she said was sensible. I could see that.

We said good night for the second time and went back to our rooms. I changed again, and crawled back into bed. But as I lay in bed, listening to the thunderstorm raging outside, I wasn't happy.

I didn't believe the nightmare story. Not for a minute. Now I knew for sure there was something really wrong. Aunt Vivien was in trouble.

I lay awake for hours, tossing and turning. The thunderstorm had long passed, and it was starting to get light by the time I fell asleep.

I'd expected to be woken early. After all, this was the country, and we were going to be working. But it was past nine o'clock when I opened my eyes. Sunlight was flooding through the thin slit of my window.

I lay there, blinking. Just for a moment, I didn't quite know where I was.

Then I remembered. The screams in the night. The storm. Mrs. Never-dead shining the flashlight in my face and ordering us back to bed.

Everything seemed terribly quiet. I got out of bed and quickly pulled on my clothes. My heart had started hammering. Where was everyone? What had happened?

But nothing had happened. Everyone had just slept in. Nick came out of his room at the same time I came out of mine, looking tired and crabby. Behind his own door, Tom was thumping around, complaining to himself as he got dressed. We waited for him, and then went down to the mezzanine, to see what the others were doing.

They were in Liz's room, talking. Just exactly as they'd been last night. Except that now it was light, and I could see the dark circles under their eyes. They'd obviously slept as poorly as we had.

"Breakfast," said Tom firmly, and they nodded.

We shuffled downstairs, hardly speaking. I glanced at the heavy carved door as we reached the room with the big round table. I wondered what had been going on behind it last night. I wondered what was going to happen today.

8

Horrors

The Never-deads, looking rather the worse for wear after their busy night, were drinking coffee at the kitchen table when we came in. When they saw us, they both stood up. Mr. Never-dead turned his back and looked out the window.

"Good morning," the woman said. "You'll find a box of cereal in the pantry, and milk in the left-hand refrigerator."

So breakfast was going to be cereal and milk. After last night, none of us had really expected a big country breakfast. But when I opened the fridge to get out the milk and saw all the goodies inside, I could have cried.

There was a leg of ham. There were eggs and bacon. There was a huge bowl of fruit salad. There were melons and grapes and bottles of orange juice. There was cream.

The pantry was stacked to the rafters with cans and packages. I turned my face away from them and sadly pulled out the giant-size box of cereal from the bottom shelf.

I carried it to the table. Sunny had already gotten bowls and spoons for everyone. Everyone else sat down and helped themselves eagerly. But I looked at Mrs. Never-dead, who was standing by the sink.

"How's Aunt Vivien?" I asked her.

"Not too bad, considering," the woman said.

"I'd like to see her, please," I said, as politely as I could. "If she's not well, I could go to her room."

Mrs. Never-dead hesitated for a moment. Then with a sigh she clattered her cup into the sink.

"That won't be necessary," she snapped. "She'll be down shortly. Just have your breakfast."

She strode out of the kitchen. Her husband stayed where he was, hands in pockets, staring out at the view.

We had two huge bowls of cereal each. We were all starving.

In a way, I wouldn't have been surprised if Mrs. Never-dead had come back saying that Aunt Vivien had gone back to sleep. For some reason she obviously wasn't eager to let me see her. But I guess she'd decided I wasn't going to quit so easily, because we'd just finished our second bowl of cereal when Aunt Vivien came in.

She looked much the same as she had yesterday, except that she was wearing sunglasses.

"The morning sun hurts your aunt's eyes," said Mrs. Never-dead, frowning at my curious look. "Isn't that right, Miss Zimmer?"

"Yes," murmured Aunt Vivien, and sniffed. Mrs. Never-dead guided her toward a chair at one end of the table, and she sank down into it as if she was exhausted.

"Good morning, Aunt Vivien," I said, as cheerily as I could.

She smiled at me and fiddled uncertainly with a loose button on her cardigan.

"Are you going to have some breakfast, Miss Zimmer?" asked Tom, seeing an opportunity for more food, and seizing it. "There's some nice-looking ham in the fridge."

Aunt Vivien turned her head to look at him. And as she did, I saw behind the side of her glasses.

I shivered in horror. The old woman had a black eye!

"I heard you call out last night," I said loudly. "I was worried about you."

Aunt Vivien opened her mouth to speak, but Mrs. Never-dead cut in with a forced laugh before she could say a word. "It was just a nightmare, wasn't it, Miss Zimmer?"

Aunt Vivien's shoulders slumped, and she nodded silently.

I saw the Never-deads exchanging meaningful looks.

"Well," said the man, "time for you kids to get to work. Weeding the front yard. Right?"

Aunt Vivien was staring down at the tabletop.

"Aunt Vivien . . ." I began. But she didn't offer any sign that she'd heard me.

Sunny tugged at my arm. "Let's go, Elmo," she muttered.

I met her eyes. They were serious and watchful. And they were sending me a message.

I saw what you saw, those eyes were saying. *Let's get out where we can talk.*

We went out to the front yard and started pulling out weeds. Mr. Never-dead watched us for a while, then wandered off.

As soon as we were alone, Sunny and I told the others about Aunt Vivien's black eye.

"Maybe she got it falling out of bed," Tom suggested.

I shook my head. "I don't think so. It didn't look just like an ordinary cut or a bruise."

Sunny nodded her agreement.

"But they couldn't really have been *harming* her, could they?" breathed Richelle. "I mean, she's just an old lady."

"It happens," I said grimly. "She might have bruises on her arms and legs as well, hidden under her clothes."

"But why?" frowned Nick. "Why would they be hurting her?"

I shivered. "I don't know. All I know is, she's scared to death of them. You can see it. That woman talks for her. Won't let her be alone with us. And Aunt Vivien doesn't even try. Those two have got her completely beaten."

"This is *terrible*," Liz hissed. "What are we going to do?"

"Whatever it is, we'll have to be careful," said Sunny. "We don't want to make things worse for her."

"Maybe we should wait till we get home, and then tell Zim," Richelle put in.

"We won't be getting home till Monday afternoon, Richelle!" Liz exploded. "We can't leave her in this situation till then."

"We've got to get her alone," I said. "Talk to her. Find out what's going on. Tell her we'll help her."

"Yeah," Tom agreed. "But that means getting rid of the Never-deads. And that's not going to be easy."

We spread out and started pulling weeds again. We worked for five minutes without stopping. But all the time we were moving farther and farther away from the kitchen side of the house. Eventually, we knew, we'd be out of sight. Then we could talk properly.

I looked up after a while and saw that Nick was beckoning to me. With a quick glance at the kitchen door — all clear — I ran over to him.

Nick was holding a piece of paper. It had been crumpled up, but he'd flattened it out again. He held it out to me.

It was a poster about Saturday night's wrestling match. Exactly like the one Tom had decorated at the Kneebone station. Except that this one was stained, and it had none of Tom's improvements.

I frowned at Nick as the others gathered around to see what he was showing me.

"So?" I asked him.

"So look at that," he said impatiently, and flicked the paper with his finger. "What does it say?"

I read the words under the pictures of the Roman gladiator and the monster man sizing up one another.

THE KILLER vs. THE FREAK

TWO DEADLY ENEMIES LOCKED IN FIGHT TO THE DEATH.

KNEEBONE TOWN HALL, SATURDAY NIGHT.
BE THERE!

"What's the big deal?" asked Tom, looking over my shoulder. "A poster smeared with tomato sauce."

"I found it just now, on the grass by the wall of the house," Nick said.

"Maybe Mr. Never-dead planned to go to the match," Tom said. "But now that he's getting his kicks from beating up old ladies, he's lost interest. We should get him for littering."

"Yes," said Richelle. "The pig! And he dropped it this morning, too. I cleaned up around the tower yesterday. No way I would have missed it."

"Look, you dopes, Never-dead didn't drop this! Can't you see?" Nick stabbed at the paper impatiently.

I looked at the grubby paper again, and suddenly I saw what he meant. The tomato sauce marks formed a pattern. They'd been carefully smeared on the paper, probably by someone's finger.

Some of the words had been highlighted. They leaped out at me, glowing red. And they were followed by a ragged "V."

I noticed something else, too. Something that made my stomach turn over.

"It's a message," breathed Liz. "And that drip-mark there at the end of the middle line. It's a 'V,' isn't it?"

"Yes," I said grimly. "'V' for Vivien."

Liz looked closely at the paper and sniffed.

When she looked up again, she had a curious expression on her face.

"You know, this doesn't smell like tomato sauce," she said slowly.

I shook my head. I felt sick.

"That's because it's not tomato sauce," I said grimly.

9

The plan

"She's sent us a coded message," I continued. I was proud of Aunt Vivien just then. I'd said the Never-deads had her beaten. But they didn't.

They were stopping her from asking us for help directly. But she'd found a way of doing it secretly. It must have taken a lot of courage. She was a real Zimmer all right, whatever Grandad had thought.

"See?" I pointed to the words that had been smeared with blood. "It's the middle line that's been marked."

Liz read the glowing, highlighted words and the signature that followed.

TWO DEADLY ENEMIES . . .
FIGHT TO THE DEATH. V.

There was a short, breathless silence as we took this in.

"Well, we know one thing now," Sunny said, after a moment. "These people aren't just playing around."

"How did she get hold of the poster, do you think?" asked Richelle.

"I reckon it must have fallen out of old Never-dead's pocket," Tom said.

"So she found it, and got away somewhere on her own. Then she marked the poster and tossed it out of one of the upstairs windows, hoping we'd find it," Liz said. "A bathroom window, maybe. They'd let her go to the bathroom alone, surely."

We all looked up. And high above us there was a small window, right near the top of the tower.

"I can't believe this is really happening," moaned Richelle.

I crumpled up the note and stuffed it into my pocket. I was shaking all over. It was shock, I suppose. And anger. And pity for this poor, terrified old lady I hardly knew, but who'd been my own grandad's little sister.

"We've got to do something," I said, through gritted teeth. "And we have to let her know we've gotten her message."

"We will, Elmo," Liz said, putting an arm around my shoulders. "But we must not panic. We have to plan."

We moved a bit farther away from the house. We kept pulling weeds, so we'd look as though we were still working. But we stood close enough to each other to talk.

"Okay. Now. We can't all just disappear and rush off to get help at Kneebone," Sunny said. "The Never-deads might suspect something. They might . . . hurt her again."

I winced. But I knew she was right.

"We have to pretend we don't know anything," I agreed.

"So we split up," Liz put in. "We send one person into town to get help, and cover for him, or her. Pretend that person's still here. Sunny's the best runner, so she should be it."

"She shouldn't go alone," Nick objected.

"She'll have to," I said. "It'll be hard enough covering for one person. We'd never cover for two or more."

"I'll be fine," said Sunny calmly. "But how are you going to make sure they don't realize I've gone?"

"You can pretend to be sick, or faint or something," suggested Liz. "We could pretend to take you up to your bedroom to sleep. . . ."

"So they think I'm in my room while I climb out of a window and take off for town," Sunny chimed in.

"I still think someone should go with you," Nick insisted.

"We've been through that!" I snapped, impatient at the delay. "The rest of us have things to do here. We have to fool the Neverdeads, and we have to protect Aunt Vivien."

"It's not going to be easy," said Liz doubtfully.

"Well, if this group can't do it, no one can," I said. "Nick and Richelle are good at being nice and well-mannered to people when they don't mean it —"

"Thanks a lot," drawled Nick. But Richelle smiled. She took it as a compliment.

"Tom's good at acting —" I went on.

"Lying, you mean," Nick interrupted.

"I learn all the best things from you," Tom said.

"And," I said, raising my voice, "Liz is the perfect person to make Aunt Vivien feel better. She's good with old people. And she's good at comforting."

Liz looked at me sideways. She wasn't sure if she wanted to be seen as Little Miss Comforter.

"What about you?" she demanded.

"Oh, General Elmo will direct operations from his bed," Nick said.

"While eating ice cream," Tom added.

"And wearing silk PJs," Richelle said.

"I'll find something to do," I said, and managed to laugh, though I didn't feel much like it. I knew they were trying to make me feel better.

"So. When do we do this?" asked Sunny.

"Soon," I said. "But I think we ought to work up to it."

"That's right," Liz agreed enthusiastically. "We really want the Never-deads to believe you're sick, Sunny. So let's go inside and get them into the mood."

"I'm not much good at acting," said Sunny doubtfully.

"It's easy," exclaimed Richelle. "All you have to do is think about being sick. Tell yourself you feel faint and woozy and that you look pale and everything. And before you know it, you will! I do it all the time. When I want to."

"Me, too," agreed Tom.

Sunny glanced at them in disbelief.

Liz sighed. "Just keep quiet, and try to pretend you're very, very tired, Sunny," she said. "We'll do the rest."

We went cautiously into the kitchen. The Never-deads weren't there.

But luck was on our side. We got to the kitchen just in time to overhear a very interesting conversation.

The Never-deads were in the next room, and couldn't see us. They were talking. And we could hear every word.

"Now, don't lose your nerve, Kevin," Mrs. Never-dead was saying. "Once we get those kids out of here, there'll be nothing to worry about."

"I s'pose so," he said. "But the old lady's a toughie."

"Toughie, nothing," Mrs. Never-dead said. "She's an old woman. She'll crack in the end."

"Maybe," Mr. Never-dead said. "But we don't want those bratty kids getting antsy and telling their parents."

"Right," she agreed. "And speaking of antsy, it's about time Aunt Vivien made another appearance. Otherwise, they *will* start to wonder. We'll call them in for some morning tea, and I'll bring her down."

"It's a bit risky," Mr. Never-dead grumbled.

"Don't *worry*, Kevin," snapped the woman. "I'll be with them every second."

"What if they see that black eye?"

"They won't. Everything'll be okay as long as we don't leave them alone," Mrs. Never-dead said. "It'll take only five minutes — enough to satisfy them. Then we'll send them off to do another job. We'll work them hard all day. Give them so much to do they can't think about anything."

We heard their footsteps walking away. And slowly their voices faded. They'd gone to another part of the house.

"What *can* they be after?" Liz asked, looking at me.

"I've got no idea," I said. "But Aunt Vivien has got money. At least, Grandad always said she had. Maybe it's that."

"Maybe the Never-deads want her to change her will in their favor," Tom said.

"Or maybe there's something valuable hidden in the house," Richelle suggested. "You know. Fabulous jewelry. They could be trying to make her tell them where it is."

"Or there could be something on the land. Or under it," Nick said. "Oil. Gold. A diamond mine. Something like that. And they're wanting her to sell the land to them."

"It doesn't really matter what they want, does it?" I broke in. "What matters is that they're dangerous."

"Aunt Vivien should have been more careful who she hired," said Tom.

"I don't think she did," I said flatly. "I don't think they're really Aunt Vivien's housekeeper and farm manager."

"I've been thinking the same thing," said Nick. "For a start, they couldn't have been here very long, or they'd have known about the trains."

"Yes," said Liz. "And if the Never-deads were real house-help, Aunt Vivien wouldn't need us to get the yard and stuff all tidied up. Would she?"

"And what about the letters?" Tom added. "They obviously hadn't seen those. Or they'd have known we were coming. So they must have come here since Aunt Vivien got Zim's last letter. Only a couple of days ago."

"And she wouldn't have told them about us," I put in. "We were her last chance of being rescued. Looks like we got here just in time."

The kitchen door swung open. Mr. Never-dead stood there, scowling at us.

"Just in time?" he said angrily. "What do you mean by that?"

10

Finders keepers

The man strode into the kitchen. My throat went dry. How much had he heard?

"What d'you mean, 'just in time'?" he repeated.

"I —" I hesitated. I didn't know what to say.

"Yeah. We came in just in time to stop ourselves from dying of thirst," grinned Tom, ambling over to the sink as if he didn't have a worry in the world.

I couldn't help admiring him. Call it acting, or call it lying, he was very good at it.

"Oh, right," growled Mr. Never-dead.

He looked behind him, then stood aside to let his wife lead Aunt Vivien into the room.

"Sit down, Miss Zimmer," said the woman with that terrible, fake smile. She pushed Aunt Vivien down onto one of the kitchen chairs. "Now. Would you like a nice cup of tea?"

Aunt Vivien nodded. "Yes, please," she said in a low voice.

"The children have been working very hard," chattered Mrs. Never-dead, filling the kettle at the sink. "They've been doing some weeding this morning."

"Oh, that's nice," whispered the old woman. She sniffed and dabbed her nose with what looked like the same crumpled tissue she'd been using yesterday.

She looked so sad and uncomfortable. She kept looking at me, nervously, pretending to smile.

I smiled back. Then I thought of a way to let her know we'd picked up her message.

"We were thinking," I said, in a chatty sort of way. "We might all go to the amateur wrestling match at Kneebone tonight. Wouldn't that be fun?"

"Wrestling?" Richelle sneered. "Dirty, ugly, sweaty wrestlers half-killing each other? Fun?"

"Yeah, fun," Tom growled, giving Richelle a little kick in the ankle.

"Maybe Aunt Vivien would like to come, too," I said. "If she's feeling better."

For the first time, Aunt Vivien's eyes brightened and she smiled properly. It was just a little smile. But I knew she'd gotten the message.

"Of course Miss Zimmer wouldn't want to go," Mrs. Never-dead snorted. "And she couldn't walk all that way, even if she did."

"I don't think we should go, either," said Liz casually. "Sunny's not feeling too well. Are you, Sunny?"

Sunny self-consciously shook her head.

Mrs. Never-dead frowned. "What's the matter with you?" she asked Sunny sharply.

Sunny looked down at her hands.

"She might be getting the flu," said Tom. "There's a lot of it going around."

Mrs. Never-dead's frown deepened. "I hope not," she scowled. "That would be *very* inconvenient."

"I think they ought to get on with the work now," Mr. Never-dead urged, looking at her. He was getting edgy. He wanted us out of the kitchen. Away from Aunt Vivien.

His wife clicked her tongue impatiently, but nodded. "Yes," she said. "Miss Zimmer needs a bit of peace to drink her tea. You people pop back outside and clean out the Rolls garage. Off you go now."

Mr. Never-dead opened the back door, and we filed through. I managed to give Aunt Vivien another smile as I passed her.

At least, I thought, *she knows now that we're on to them. And that we'll do something to help.*

As soon as we were outside, Mr. Never-dead hustled us around to the back of the house and pointed at the garage. "Okay," he growled. "You'd better get started. And no messing around. There's lots more work for you to do before the day's over."

He was right there. But it wasn't the sort of work he had in mind.

The back of the garage was piled high with junk. Bits of old beds. Rusty paint tins. Piles of old newspapers and magazines. You name it, Aunt Vivien had stuck it in the garage. There were also the shelves of papers that climbed up the side walls to the roof.

"Clear out the whole garage," said Mr. Never-dead. "We'll sort through it later."

He pointed to a clear space in the yard. "You can pile it up out there. And you can clean the Rolls while you're at it."

So we started doing what he said. We lugged all the stuff from the back of the garage first. It was awkward because we had to edge around the Rolls to get outside. But little by little a junk heap started building up.

When the back of the garage was clear, Richelle and Sunny and I started cleaning the car. The others went on moving papers from the shelves.

The Rolls was really beautiful. What a shame it was going to waste. It was huge, probably fifty years old. It could have fit all of us and a few more.

Somehow or other Richelle had managed to organize things so she was cleaning the inside of the car. She always seems to get the good jobs.

"It's great," she called through the back window. "Real leather seats. Oh, imagine driving around in a car like this!"

"Get on with it, Richelle," Liz ordered. She turned to Sunny. "And you," she said softly. "Don't work so hard. Look droopy. You're supposed to be feeling sick. We should make our move soon."

"There's a place for champagne here!" chattered Richelle. "And an adorable little wooden cupboard in the back of the front seats. That must be for glasses. See? Oh!"

She squealed as a wooden flap swung smoothly down from the cabinet, to make a shelf.

"Richelle!" exclaimed Liz impatiently.

But Richelle was frowning and pulling something from the cupboard.

"What is it?" I asked, bending to look.

She held it out to show me.

It was a small gold-colored box. It was an oval shape and had four little legs shaped to look like the legs on an old-fashioned chair. It had a lacy design around the edges and a rose design on the lid. A key was tied to one of its legs with a piece of narrow ribbon.

"Isn't it gorgeous?" Richelle said. "Well, this isn't going out with the junk, that's for sure."

"Open it!" Liz said eagerly, coming to look.

Richelle tried, but the box was fastened shut. And, strangely, she couldn't make the key on the end of the ribbon fit the lock.

"It's the wrong key," she said in disappointment.

"It can't be. Let me try," I said.

Richelle handed the box over, and I tried the key myself. But I couldn't make it work, either. All I managed to do was make the old ribbon fall apart.

"It's probably the right key, but the lock's rusted up," Tom said.

I gave the box back to Richelle. She gazed at it, smiling to herself.

"I wonder if Aunt Vivien would let me keep it," she murmured. "I mean, after this is all over, maybe you could ask her, Elmo. . . ."

A booming voice from the garage door made us all jump.

"I'll take that!"

It was Mr. Never-dead.

He pointed to Richelle, who was hiding her little treasure behind her back.

"Come on, give it here." He held out his hand.

Richelle hesitated for a moment, then shrugged and sulkily passed over the box.

"Where did you find it?" he demanded, turning it over in his hands.

"In the car," muttered Richelle.

"Was there anything in it?"

She shrugged. "You can't open it," she said.

"Oh, yes, I can," he grinned. "Now you children finish your work, and stop gabbing!"

With that, he rushed back to the house. He was obviously excited. And as we watched him go, we couldn't help wondering if the box, or what was inside it, was the key to the whole mystery.

"They've been looking for something, all right," murmured Nick. "This proves it, I'd say."

"And we found it for them," said Richelle bitterly.

I shook my head. "We don't know we've found it," I said. "It's quite possible that the little box has nothing to do with anything."

"I just wish he hadn't gotten it." Richelle was still fuming. "And I wish I'd been able to open it before he did. I wish that key had worked."

I grinned. "It might work on something else," I said. I held up the key by its broken piece of ribbon.

"He only asked for the box," I said. "So I kept this. You never know where it might fit."

And as they stared at me, I stuck the key deep into my pocket.

"Now," I said firmly, "let's start getting Sunny out of here."

11

Storm clouds

We left the garage. Liz looked up at the sky and frowned. Dark clouds had begun to roll over from the west. We could hear rumbling thunder in the distance.

"We'd better hurry," she said. "Or Sunny'll be running through pouring rain."

"Okay, let's do it," I said.

Just then, Mr. Never-dead came back into the yard carrying a roll of black plastic. He didn't look happy and excited anymore. He just looked crabby. I decided that he'd already investigated the little gold-covered box and discovered that it didn't contain what he wanted after all.

"Yakking again instead of working!" he yelled at us. "How many times do you have to be told to get on with it?"

"Sunny's really not feeling well," I said. "Like we said, she's probably getting the flu. She has to go inside and lie down."

The man sighed deeply. "Great," he grumbled. "That's all we need."

But he didn't say any more as Liz led Sunny toward the

house. He turned on us instead, and thrust the roll of plastic into my hands.

"Get this pile of stuff covered up quickly," he snapped. "There's going to be a storm. Hold the plastic down with some rocks and make sure no rain gets in."

"What's the point?" Richelle asked. "Isn't it all just junk?"

"I told you. We've got to go through it before we can chuck it. And I don't want it soaking wet."

So . . . the box hadn't been what the Never-deads were after. The search was still definitely on. Good.

While Mr. Never-dead stomped back to the house, we started wrestling with the black plastic. The wind had really revved up.

I crouched down to roll some rocks onto the plastic nearest to me. And then I happened to look up. And I saw it.

A weird, greenish light glowed and danced around the steeple and the tower.

I gasped and pointed. And then the others saw it, too.

"What is it?" shrieked Richelle.

"Saint Elmo's fire," I breathed. Shivers were running up and down my spine.

It was an awesome sight. I could just imagine how sailors must have felt in the old days, seeing that strange unearthly flicker around the masts of their ships.

"I hope it's true," I said, almost to myself.

"What?" Tom asked, still staring at the light.

"Isn't seeing Saint Elmo's fire supposed to be good luck? Isn't it supposed to mean we're being protected by Saint Elmo?" I asked.

"Yeah," Nick said. "That's the story."

"Saint Elmo versus the Never-deads," joked Tom. "Two deadly enemies fight to the death."

I shivered. I hoped it wasn't going to come to that.

○

We finished covering the heap of stuff with the plastic and then went inside. Mr. Never-dead was sitting at the kitchen table, glumly eating a ham sandwich.

There was a grumble of thunder. He twitched nervously.

Liz came in, and he glared at her. "How's your friend?" he grunted.

"Not so well," said Liz, carefully avoiding looking at us. "Anyway, I told her to try to rest. I told her she wouldn't be disturbed. Sleep should help."

"It'd better," he said rudely, and went on eating.

"Where's Mrs. . . . um . . . Everedd?" I asked. I kept forgetting Mrs. Never-dead's real name.

"I saw her in the living room just now," said Liz, raising her voice over the thunder. "She's coming out to help us get lunch."

I saw her wink fleetingly. She was letting me know that Sunny was all set to creep out the back way.

We helped ourselves to glasses of water. Tom looked longingly at the pantry. Mr. Never-dead finished his sandwich and gazed blankly out the window.

There was a long silence. I guess we were all feeling tense. Scared that Mrs. Never-dead would go back upstairs for some reason and catch Sunny sneaking out.

So it was a relief when Mrs. Never-dead appeared. It was

even a relief to see her awful smile. She didn't suspect anything, anyway. And with both of the Never-deads in the kitchen with us, Sunny would have a clear run.

Mrs. Never-dead went into the pantry and came out with some bread, a tub of margarine, and a half-used jar of peanut butter.

"Would you like a glass of milk to go with your sandwiches?" she asked.

The ham was for Mr. Never-dead's use only, it seemed.

But no one argued. We knew that we had to keep them happy. We started making sandwiches for ourselves.

The bread was stale, and the peanut butter was old and dried out. But by this time, despite all our worries, we were so hungry that we almost didn't care. And of course, we'd all said yes to the milk. It at least was fresh and icy-cold from the fridge.

By the time ten minutes had passed, we'd all started to relax. We knew that we'd given Sunny plenty of time to get away.

The thunder was still rumbling outside, and getting louder. The storm was coming closer. But there was still no rain. With a bit of luck, Sunny would have reached Kneebone before it started. Without us to hold her up it wouldn't take her too long to get there.

We'd taken as long as we could to eat, but finally there was nothing left but empty glasses, a bread wrapper, and a few tiny crumbs of bread. We took our plates, the glasses, and the empty peanut-butter jar to the sink.

"Leave them for me to do," said Mrs. Never-dead. "You go back outside and get on with the work."

We exchanged worried glances. We really didn't want to leave

Mrs. Never-dead alone in the house with Aunt Vivien. And what if she decided to check on Sunny and discovered she'd gone?

The thunder rumbled. She frowned and put her hand to her forehead.

"Do you have a headache?" asked Richelle, as though she was really interested.

The woman nodded shortly.

"That's a shame," said Richelle, sounding honestly sympathetic, though I knew that, of course, she wasn't. "My mother always gets headaches just before a storm, too. You should go and lie down before it gets any worse."

I could have cheered. *Good for you, Richelle*, I thought.

"I might do that," said Mrs. Never-dead. "Yes, I think I will."

"I could do with a bit of shut-eye myself," her husband said hopefully.

She glanced at him coldly. "It's important to keep these young people busy, Kevin," she said. "And out in the open air."

Away from Aunt Vivien, was what she meant. And, of course, he knew it. He groaned and stood up. "All right," he grunted.

We followed him outside. "You stay here," he said. "I'll be back in a minute." He went off toward the back of the house.

I picked up the empty bread wrapper from the table. I opened the garbage bin outside the back door, to throw the wrapper away. The others heard my exclamation and turned to look.

I bent over the bin to pull something out.

"Hey, Elmo, you're not *that* hungry, are you?" joked Tom.

But if they'd been thinking about laughing, they quickly stopped when I showed them what I had in my hand.

66

It was the remains of the beautiful little gold-colored box. Twisted and half-smashed, it had been pried open with something.

"Oh!" Richelle had tears in her eyes. "How could they do that!"

"I think they'd do anything," I said grimly.

I threw the box back into the bin and closed the lid.

Mr. Never-dead came back lugging some tools, a bucket, a flashlight, and a rope.

Richelle shot him a furious look. She wanted to say something about the ruined box, but, of course, she couldn't. She knew we had to play it cool.

"What are we going to do now?" drawled Nick, raising one eyebrow as he looked at the rope.

"The well," said Mr. Never-dead with a satisfied smirk. "That should keep you out of trouble."

I heard Tom groan softly beside me. I glanced quickly around at four faces filled with the same dismay I felt. The last thing any of us wanted to see was the well.

12

Down the ladder

The afternoon was gloomy as we trudged after Mr. Never-dead toward the well.

Dark clouds were rolling in from the west, packing tightly together and bunching over the house. I couldn't see Saint Elmo's fire dancing around on the roof anymore. But still, the thunder only rumbled, and no rain fell.

We reached the well, and Mr. Never-dead pulled the heavy cover to one side, with much groaning and puffing. He shone the flashlight down the yawning hole. You couldn't see much. Just the glint of metal, stones, and dirt, plus the rungs of an old iron ladder attached to the brick walls.

"It's all clogged up down there, apparently," said Mr. Never-dead, forgetting for the moment that he was supposed to be the farm manager. "Old bricks, machinery parts, some rocks, and a lot of silt. It's all got to be dug out and brought up to the top so the well can fill again."

He started tying the rope to the bucket and telling us what we were expected to do. Some of us would work at the bottom of the well, digging out the dirt and rocks and putting them in the bucket. Mr. Never-dead would haul up the bucket, empty it, then let it down again to be refilled.

"It'll be heavy," he said. "Two of you can stand on the ladder and help lift. Who's going down to dig?"

"Not me," said Tom flatly.

"Tom's claustrophobic," Liz told the man. "He can't handle closed-in spaces."

"How convenient," drawled Nick.

Tom flushed, and shot him an angry look.

"Nick, you know it's true!" Liz exclaimed.

"As long as I can look up and see out, I'll be okay," Tom said. "I'll stand on the ladder and help with the lifting."

"Well, I'm not going down that hole," Richelle said. "It's probably full of snakes and spiders and rats."

"You don't get rats and snakes together," Tom said. "Snakes eat rats."

"Yu-uuk." Richelle was nearly sick.

"Look," Liz said impatiently. "Tom's out of it. The rest of us will have to draw straws. The longest straw gets to be below Tom on the ladder; the rest go down the hole. Okay?"

Richelle agreed, hoping she'd get the long straw.

But I got it.

"Elmo," Richelle said, putting on her most helpless look. "I *can't* go down that well. Can we change places?"

"No way," I said. "Down you go, like a good brave girl."

She glared at me. In fact, if looks could kill, as Dad sometimes says, I wouldn't be telling this story.

69

"Okay," growled Mr. Never-dead. "Small stuff in the bucket. Heavy rocks to be tied securely and hauled up separately. Now stop messing around and do it already, will you?"

Nick went down first, carrying the flashlight. It didn't help much when he called out that the ladder felt like it might break any second.

Liz followed him. Then Richelle closed her eyes and went, too, with a last, thunderous look in my direction. She squeaked and squealed all the way down.

I went down next. I hung there on the ladder about halfway down, waiting for the first bucket full of junk. I could see Tom clinging to the ladder above me, and a circle of light above him. Below, the flashlight tilted around crazily. There was the sound of clattering — and more screams from Richelle.

"There's something on me!" she screeched. "It's crawling up my leg. Aaah! Get it off! Get it off! Shine the flashlight here."

"There's nothing on you, Richelle." Nick's voice echoed up to me.

"Yes, there is!"

"It's just your imagination," Liz said. "Come on. Help us, for goodness' sake. Let's get this over with."

I was very glad I'd drawn the long straw.

Up came the first bucket. Mr. Never-dead took it from Tom and moved away from the well to empty it.

"Okay, now keep it moving," he called, sending the empty bucket down again.

I wondered if the Never-deads thought something might be hidden in the well. Why else would Mr. Never-dead stay and haul out filled buckets?

It was the thought that he was after something that kept me going. The circle of sky at the top of the well was almost black now. The only light came from the flashlight, way down in the deep hole.

We must have done about five buckets when Nick called up that he was tying a rock on the rope.

"It's a big one," he said. His voice boomed around the walls of the well. "Give the rope a tug to make sure the knots hold."

Tom and I took the rope and pulled together. It seemed safe enough.

"Okay," Nick called.

We pulled and hauled at the rock. It was incredibly heavy. It was just below me when we heard a thin, angry voice calling from the house. It was Mrs. Never-dead, yelling her husband's name.

"I'm wanted back at the house," he called down to us. "Won't be long."

His face disappeared from above, and suddenly, the rock was even heavier. He'd dropped his end of the rope.

"Hey, don't leave us here with this rock halfway up!" I yelled in panic. "It's too heavy for us."

"Look, just balance it on the ladder," I heard him call. "Stay where you are. I'll be right back."

"Hey!" I yelled again. But he'd already gone.

"Come on!" Nick called from the bottom of the well. "I don't want to be down here all night. Let's go!"

Tom and I heaved on the rope together. My arms felt as though they were being pulled out of their sockets. Slowly the rock reached my feet.

"We'll try to get it onto the next rung!" I shouted to Tom. "Heave!"

We both pulled with all our strength.

And then the rope snapped.

The huge rock went crashing down, thudding into the iron rungs of the ladder as it fell.

Our screams echoed around the rough brick walls. There was a final, mighty crash. Then all was silent. Shaking all over, I looked down. There was no light and no movement.

"Liz! Nick! Richelle!" I shouted. "Are you all right?"

With enormous relief, I heard soft sobbing. Richelle. Then I heard Nick swearing to himself. So he was all right. But . . .

"Liz!" I called. My teeth were chattering. I felt numb.

"Liz!" roared Tom from above me.

"I'm here."

It was Liz's voice. Shaky and tearful, but definitely Liz's voice. My knees went weak. I clung to the ladder, trying to stop myself from shaking. For a minute I'd thought . . .

"The flashlight is broken," Liz quavered. "We can't see anything. But we're okay. We're coming up."

I could hear her urging Richelle to start climbing the ladder.

"I can't," Richelle was wailing. "My legs are too weak."

"Do you want to get out of here, or not?" roared Nick.

There was a scuffling sound.

"That's it," I heard Liz saying. "Just keep going. . . ."

"Out!" I called to Tom. "They're coming up."

He and I climbed quickly out of the well. It was blissful to breathe the fresh air again.

We lay flat on the ground, ready to take Richelle's hand and help her as soon as she got close enough.

Then she screamed.

"The ladder's gone!" she shrieked. "Liz, it's gone. It just stops. There's nothing to hold on to!"

"Let me see."

There was another scuffle, as if Liz and Richelle were changing places.

I peered down into the well, but couldn't see anything.

"What's happening?" I called.

"I — I think the rock must have crashed into the ladder and broken off some of the rungs." Liz's voice was shaking. "Elmo, we can't see anything. And . . . and I can't feel any rungs except for the first few."

"Stretch your arm up," I said. "I'll see if I can reach you."

Tom, white as paper, gripped my ankles as I slid headfirst into the well, holding on to the top rungs of the ladder. I didn't dare go too far in case I got too heavy for him and fell. I stretched out my arm as far as possible, but I couldn't feel Liz's hand.

"No luck," I finally called out. "Listen, we'll have to go for help. We'll get a ladder. I saw one leaning up against the house. And we'll get Mr. Never-dead."

Thunder — loud thunder — crashed around our heads. It was dark as night. The wind was roaring.

"Don't leave us," screamed Richelle. "What if it starts to rain? Snakes might come in. The well will fill up with water. We'll be drowned!"

Nick and Liz had also begun to panic. I could hear it in their voices. Not because of the rain. Or snakes. But it must have been terrible down there, trapped in the dark. Leaving them was one of the hardest things I've ever done in my life.

But Tom and I had to do it. And the quicker we went, the quicker we'd be able to save them.

"We'll be back," I yelled.

We scrambled to our feet — and ran.

We were halfway to the house when I thought of something.

"Sunny should be back from Kneebone with help any minute now," I panted to Tom.

"Should be," he agreed. "But we can't wait for that, can we?"

He was sweating. And it wasn't the running. He'd broken out in a sweat just thinking about being stuck in that well.

The kitchen door at the back of the house was open, and I almost ran straight in, yelling for help. I can't say why I stopped. Just one of those things, I guess.

Afterward, I thought of Saint Elmo's fire. The sign of protection. Because if I hadn't hesitated, and heard the Never-deads arguing inside the house, I hate to think what would have happened.

I grabbed Tom by the arm and pulled him back from the doorway.

"Shhhh," I whispered. "Listen."

"You've got no choice," Mrs. Never-dead was shouting. "Just do as I say."

"I won't. You're going too far," he shouted back. "I never —"

"I tell you, those kids are on to us," she broke in savagely. "They've got to be disposed of! We'll see to the little sickly one upstairs later. Go on! Do it!"

13

Rescue

Tom and I shrank back from the doorway.

"All right!" we heard the man yell. "All right!"

His footsteps raced toward the door. We turned and ran around to the back of the house.

The ladder was standing there, against the wall. We peered around the house corner and saw Mr. Never-dead stomping off toward the well.

"I don't believe this," Tom whispered. "They're going to kill us. They're not just con artists or treasure hunters. They're murderers!"

I thought rapidly. We assumed we'd done well pretending we knew nothing! Obviously, it hadn't worked. Somehow, Mrs. Never-dead had caught on.

"Come on," I urged. "Get the other end of the ladder."

We staggered around to the other side of the house with the ladder held between us. We kept low, diving as quickly as we could among the overgrown bushes. Never-dead stopped at the well. There was a chorus of muffled shouts and screams. Liz, Nick, and Richelle must have seen his shape looming over them.

Tom and I put the ladder down and lay flat. My heart was pounding.

"We've got to do something quickly," Tom whispered.

"We can't tackle him," I said. "He's pretty strong. He'd end up catching us, too."

"I wish Sunny was here," Tom said. "Then we'd show him."

"She's better where she is," I said. "Getting help. We fooled them about that, anyhow. They think she's still upstairs."

"What do you think he's going to do?" Tom said through chattering teeth. "What if he shoots them?"

"He won't do that, even if he's got a gun."

"Why not? You heard what she said."

"Yeah. But that would look like murder, when the bodies were found. I think he's going to organize an accident."

"You mean —"

Tom's voice dried up as he saw what the man was doing. His whole body went rigid.

"He's putting the lid on the well," he hissed. "Elmo, he's —"

I gripped his arm. "It'll be okay," I said. "Hey, Tom, it's okay. Old Never-dead's got one big problem. He thinks we're *all* down there."

Tom's teeth showed in a shaky grin. "Yeah," he said. Then the smile disappeared. "How could anyone do that?" he muttered. "Just cover that hole and leave them to — Oh, Elmo . . . they're screaming."

He'd started shaking again. He clapped his hands over his ears. I gritted my teeth.

The screams were horrible. It was awful to think of Liz, Nick, and Richelle going through this. But I knew that the noise they were making was a good thing.

They were yelling loudly enough for ten people. It fooled Never-dead completely. He didn't even bother to look down the well, to check that we were all there. Not that he could have seen much in that blackness. But he didn't even try.

He finished putting the heavy wooden lid over the well, and suddenly, everything was quiet. You couldn't hear the voices anymore.

Mr. Never-dead rolled a huge rock onto the well lid to weigh it down. Tom stared at me. I stared at him. We were both in shock, I think. Because we realized now, more than ever, the terrible truth.

If we'd been down that well with the others, no one would have known. Sunny would have come back with help and been told that we'd left. Aunt Vivien wouldn't know any different.

Without us to back her up, Sunny's story would have sounded wild — a teenage kid's hysterics. And without us around to support her, Aunt Vivien might easily have been too scared to tell the police the truth about the Never-deads.

So in the well we probably would have stayed. By the time a search for us was started, it would have been too late. We would have died of thirst or suffocation in the blackness.

That was the terrible truth. And it frightened us just thinking about it.

It was dark as night as we lay there, waiting for the man to leave. The wind had dropped. The air was electric. The only light came from the house windows — and the weird, green glow of Saint Elmo's fire.

And then, suddenly, the sound of the generator died away, and the lights winked out. But the green fire around the tower stayed.

Mr. Never-dead straightened up and turned around. He saw that the lights were out. He swore under his breath and began stumbling over the rough ground, toward the house.

We waited a couple of agonizing minutes, then got up on our knees and crawled to the well, dragging the ladder.

We pushed the heavy rock away and lifted the cover aside. Inside the well there was dead silence.

"It's okay, it's us," I whispered. "Tom and Elmo."

Richelle began to sob helplessly. Her voice began to rise.

"No! Hey, Richelle, keep very quiet," I hissed. "He might come back."

As quickly as we could, Tom and I extended the ladder and lowered it into the dark, gaping hole.

It wasn't long enough. Tom again held my ankles, and I lowered myself as far as I could go, holding the ladder against the side of the well. It still didn't reach the bottom.

"I can't get it down any farther," I called in a low voice.

After a few seconds, Nick answered, sounding as calm as if he was solving a computer problem back in his bedroom in Raven Hill.

"It's okay," he said. "I can just reach the bottom rung. I'll hold on to it, and the girls can get onto my shoulders and climb. Ready?"

I braced myself, and in a few seconds, I felt a weight moving slowly toward me.

I can't tell you how pleased I was when Richelle's tousled

fair head appeared out of that inky blackness. I grabbed her hand and hauled her out.

"You're okay now," I said.

She collapsed onto the ground beside Tom and sobbed quietly to herself. Just like I used to do when I was a little kid, after I'd had a nightmare or been hurt.

Liz was next — pale and streaked with mud, and with a cut over one eye. But looking steady as a rock. She knelt down beside me. And only then did I realize that she was shaking all over.

"I'm not sure how Nick's going to make it, Elmo," she whispered.

"Are you okay, Nick?" I called.

"I'm just tying the end of the ladder with the broken rope off the bucket. I'll jump for it. You'll have to hold it steady while I climb. Can you do that?"

"Yes," I said.

He didn't say, "Don't let me fall." He didn't say, "Hold on." He just did exactly what he'd said he'd do, and he trusted me to do the same.

Liz helped me hold the ladder. Richelle and Tom held on to us. And one terrifying minute later, Nick was crawling, exhausted, onto the grass beside us.

We all hugged each other with relief. I looked up at the dark house. Saint Elmo's fire was still flickering around the tower and the spire.

"We've got Saint Elmo's protection," I said.

"Well, it's worked so far," muttered Nick. "Let's hope he keeps it up."

We covered the well again and rolled the heavy rock back

over it. Now, if Mr. Never-dead came to check, there'd be nothing to show that anything had changed.

The lightning flashed, the thunder crashed, and at last, the rain came down. We scuttled off into the bushes, to get some shelter and talk about what we should do next.

And then we remembered Sunny.

"Where *is* she?" Liz exclaimed.

"Something terrible's happened to her on the road. I just know it." Richelle wiped her eyes with the back of her hand. Her hair was hanging in rats' tails on her shoulders. She was being rained on, and she didn't even care.

"I told you she shouldn't have gone alone," muttered Nick.

"Listen, Sunny can look after herself," said Tom. "She's got more guts and more muscles than the rest of us put together."

Liz nodded, grinning shakily. But you could see that she was still worried.

"I vote we sneak out of here as fast as we can and get to Kneebone," said Nick.

But I shook my head. "I'm not going," I said, raising my voice over the thunder. "I can't leave Aunt Vivien alone in the house with those two killers. I've got to get her out."

They tried to talk me out of it, but I wouldn't be budged.

"All right. We'll all stay. One for all, all for one," sighed Liz.

"I'm not in," whispered Richelle. "I just don't want to be out on my own."

I felt a pang, looking at her frightened face. She'd been through something shocking. And I was making her stay in danger. I was making them all stay.

"You go, and leave me here," I said. "I'll be okay. Really."

"Oh, sure, Saint Elmo," jeered Tom. "You'll be fine. You'll just break into that house, knock out the Never-deads with a single blow, and carry Aunt Vivien six miles into Kneebone in the middle of a thunderstorm all on your own. Won't you?"

I had to laugh. Of course, he was right.

"Okay, then," said Nick. "We go back to the house. We sneak in. We find Aunt Vivien. We get her out."

Richelle shivered. "The house is pitch-black," she said, peering through the bushes. "What's happening over there?"

"The generator seems to have gone off," I said. "It should make things a bit easier."

"Or harder," said Nick. "Depends on how you look at it."

14

Attack and defense

The rain had started to ease as we crept toward the dark house. We were all cold and soaked through. As we drew closer, we could hear the sound of metal hitting metal, and voices arguing.

"The generator shed," breathed Tom.

We peered around the corner of the house.

The flashlight in the generator shed was weak and flickering, but showed that the Never-deads were both there. Mrs. Never-dead was giving her husband a hard time.

"It's run out of fuel," she snapped. "Hasn't it?"

"It had, but I just filled it. Now it's clogged, or something."

"You should have filled it before it ran out."

"It's not my job."

"That's no answer!"

"Get off my back, will you? Hold the flashlight still!"

As quickly and quietly as we could, we turned and ran around the front of the house and let ourselves in the kitchen door, bolting it behind us. Nick ran to the front door and secured the bolts there, too.

"That'll slow them up a bit," he said as he reunited with us in the dark kitchen.

It was still pitch-dark. But the regular flashes of lightning helped as we felt our way to the heavy, carved door in the room just below our bedrooms.

The Never-deads had told us that "Miss Zimmer's private quarters" were behind that door. And the screams in the night had come from behind that door, too. For sure Aunt Vivien was being kept prisoner in there.

"Do you think we can break it down?" I whispered.

Nick frowned. "I doubt it," he said. "We'll have to find another way. Maybe we could pick the lock with —"

Liz stretched out her hand and turned the handle.

And like magic, the door opened. It was unlocked!

Nick lifted an eyebrow.

"I thought it was worth trying," Liz said, as if she was apologizing for spoiling his plans. "You never know."

A dark hallway loomed in front of us.

We felt our way along in the darkness. We reached some steps and climbed them, alert for any sound, any trace of movement.

"I think we're going toward the tower," whispered Nick.

At the top of the steps was a door.

"The tower room," whispered Liz. "She's in the tower room. Of course! The note was thrown from there."

So far, so good, I thought. Then I froze.

"Listen," I whispered.

We all heard a groan. It was coming through the tower room door. I felt my stomach tense up.

Don't panic, I told myself. *If it's Aunt Vivien, at least she's still alive.*

The door was unlocked. The hinges creaked as I slowly opened it. I felt as though I was suffocating.

The windows were only slits, but as we crept through the door, the lightning flashed and briefly lit the room.

It had curved walls. It was big, but there was hardly anything in it. Just a bed and a big cupboard thing.

Then the lightning flashed again, and Richelle screamed. My stomach turned over.

Aunt Vivien was lying on the floor. She was mumbling and groaning. Her eyes were closed. Her hands and feet were tied together. And there was a huge lump on her forehead.

Fumbling in the dark, jumping with every crash of thunder, we untied Aunt Vivien and lifted her onto the bed. She was heavier than she looked.

She mumbled and raised her hand to her head. A cold anger filled me. The helpless old woman had been knocked out.

I wondered desperately how we were going to get her away from Mistfall now.

"She's been hurt," whispered Tom, looking sick.

There was a sliding door set into one of the walls. Liz looked inside and found a small bathroom.

"That's probably where she dropped the note from," she said. She went into the bathroom, ran water, and came back with a wet towel. She sat down on the bed and started cleaning Aunt Vivien's forehead.

I stood there watching helplessly.

"We can't move her in this state," said Nick, putting my thoughts into words. "Even if she wakes up, she'll be groggy. And she's too heavy for us to carry far."

"We'll have to lock ourselves in here with her and just hold out till help arrives," I said. "Sunny can't be much longer."

The others could see that this was the only answer. None of us liked it, but we had no real choice.

We couldn't find a key for the door, but I thought of another idea.

"That big dresser thing," I said. "Let's push it against the door."

"It's called a lowboy," Liz said.

Like Aunt Vivien, the lowboy was heavier than it looked. Heaving and panting, we finally managed to push it against the door.

"That should hold it," I said with satisfaction. I turned back to the bed. Liz was still cleaning Aunt Vivien's forehead with cool water.

"She's starting to wake up," she said.

"Hit me . . ." Aunt Vivien mumbled. "Head . . ."

"Just lie still," Liz soothed. "It's all right. We're here."

But Aunt Vivien tossed her head from side to side on the pillow. Her eyelids flickered as she struggled to open her eyes.

"That woman . . . a devil," she moaned. "They're in it together . . . dangerous. . . . the girl . . . look out!"

Nick looked at me. "Did you hear what she said?" he muttered.

I nodded, feeling sick.

Nick knelt down beside the bed. "What girl?" he whispered urgently to the groaning woman. "What girl do you mean?"

"Leave her alone," protested Liz. "Let her rest."

Nick ignored her. "What girl?" he urged.

"Athletic girl," she mumbled. "Trying to get away . . ."

I heard Tom and Richelle gasp in shock. Saw Liz press her hand to her mouth. Saw Nick's grim face. She was talking about Sunny.

They'd caught Sunny before she even left the house.

"What happened? Where is she? Where is she?" Liz bent over the bed, tears filling her eyes.

"Don't know. . . . Gone. . . . She was here. Tied up. My head . . ."

Aunt Vivien was struggling to get up. In the end, we helped her. She sat up on the edge of the bed, bent over with her head in her hands.

"You know what this means," Nick said.

We all did, of course. We were paralyzed with shock.

Sunny wouldn't be bringing help from town. All the time we thought she was running to Kneebone she was here, locked in the tower room.

I remembered Mrs. Never-dead telling her husband they'd take care of the "sickly" girl upstairs later. We thought we'd fooled her. We thought she still believed Sunny was asleep in her locked bedroom.

But that wasn't what it was, at all. Mrs. Never-dead had

Sunny tied up in the tower room. Somehow, she'd caught Sunny trying to sneak out — after we'd already gone to the well. And that was what made her realize we were on to them, and had to be disposed of.

What had they done to Sunny?

Richelle began to sob again. Liz put an arm around her.

"They can't get us, Richelle," she whispered. "We're safe in here."

"It's not that," sobbed Richelle. "It's . . . Sunny. Oh, Liz! They must have —"

I saw Liz's hand clench. I knew what she was feeling. It was what we were all feeling. Sunny —

Another flash. But this time it was the lights going on. We immediately turned off the light in the tower room. Somehow, the darkness made us feel safer.

"So. They've fixed the generator. They'll be coming back to the house in a minute. Or trying to," said Nick grimly. "They'll realize the doors are bolted from the inside. They'll know something's wrong."

"They'll get in here in the end," muttered Tom. "Through a window or something. The locked doors'll only slow them up. Then I'd say they'll be coming straight up here."

"We'll keep them out," I heard myself saying, in a hard voice that didn't sound like mine.

I glanced behind me at the hunched, swaying figure of Aunt Vivien sitting on the bed.

"We'll keep them out," I said again, more loudly, so she'd hear me. "We'll just stay here. And eventually someone'll come looking for us."

✿

We waited. The thunder crashed; the lightning lit up the room in brief flashes.

"When they come," I said, "they'll try to break down the door. But the lowboy's very heavy. All we have to do is put our own weight against it and we'll be okay."

"I hope you're right," murmured Tom.

"I can't stand this waiting!" whispered Richelle. "I can't stand it!"

But she didn't have to wait for much longer. Just a few minutes later, we heard banging feet and shouting voices outside the room.

The Never-deads were coming.

"I don't know, I tell you!" Mr. Never-dead shouted.

The doorknob rattled as it was twisted from the outside. Then we heard the jingling of keys as he tried a few in the lock.

"There's something fishy about this," he said at last.

"Let me try!" snapped his wife. We heard the clatter as the doorknob was twisted again.

"It's not locked, you buffoon!" screeched Mrs. Never-dead. "There's something holding it shut from inside."

They began to beat and kick at the door.

"Push, you idiot," ordered the woman. "Harder!"

But with the lowboy against it and the five of us putting our weight against the lowboy, they didn't have a chance.

I turned around to Aunt Vivien. She was on her feet and coming over to help us.

"It's okay," I whispered to her. "Don't worry. It's working. They're not going to get in."

"Now!" screeched Mrs. Never-dead from outside.

This time they must have backed away a bit and thrown themselves at the door. There was a huge crash. The door shuddered. But the lowboy held.

Then I felt two strong hands close around my throat from behind, and a voice snarled: "Let them in or I'll break his scrawny neck."

It was Aunt Vivien.

The hands tightened. I choked, fighting for breath, helpless in that iron grip. I saw the shocked faces of the others, turning to look at me. Then I could only see a red haze. I couldn't breathe. . . . I couldn't believe it. . . . I couldn't think. . . .

I heard the lowboy being moved away from the door.

Aunt Vivien let me go. I collapsed onto the floor, coughing, gasping for breath.

The Never-deads burst into the room.

And they both had weapons.

15

Saint Elmo's fire

The Never-deads grabbed me by the arm, hauled me to my feet, and threw me into the corner with the others. Mr. Never-dead switched on the light. He was waving a long lead pipe.

I was still choking and gasping. My throat felt swollen. My head was spinning.

Mrs. Never-dead was shaking Aunt Vivien roughly by the arm. "What happened?" she was screeching. "Quickly!"

"Gone," said Aunt Vivien. Her voice was still shaky. "I don't know where. It's — it's not my fault. . . ."

I just couldn't understand what was happening. Why had Aunt Vivien done this to me, to us? Why?

"Brainless idiot," growled Mr. Never-dead.

His wife turned on him. "Look who's talking!" she spat. She pointed viciously at us with a crowbar, which she had taken from the garage. "What are they doing here?"

"I put the cover on the well, just like you said," Mr. Never-dead whined. "So don't blame me. I don't know how they got out."

"Well, it doesn't matter, anyway," she said. "They're going back in. And this time we'll do it properly."

"We'll never get away with it," Mr. Never-dead moaned.

"Why shouldn't we?" Mrs. Never-dead interrupted him. "We'll take the lid off again when it's all over. Everyone'll think they went wandering off in the storm and fell down the well in the dark. We'll say we didn't look for them because we just assumed they'd gotten sick of things here and gone home."

"But you're forgetting —?" he began.

"I'm forgetting nothing!" she snapped. "She's no danger to us if we keep our wits about us."

My heart thudded. "Sunny!" I whispered. "She got away."

Liz's eyes shone. "She's alive," she breathed.

It was like being given a wonderful gift. In our hearts we'd all thought Sunny was gone forever. But she wasn't. And — I guess we all thought the same thing at the same moment — while she was alive and free, we still had a chance.

"Sunny's a really fast runner!" Richelle squeaked. "She'll be on her way to Kneebone right now, to get help. And you'll never, never catch her on foot."

Mrs. Never-dead sneered.

"D'you really think we'd let ourselves be stuck out here with no car?" she said, and sniffed. "Think we're as stupid as you are?"

Aunt Vivien just stood there. I remembered Grandad saying Aunt Vivien was unworthy of the Zimmer name. *But she is a Zimmer,* I thought. *I can't believe my own flesh and blood would do this.*

"What's the matter with you, Aunt Vivien?" I burst out. "Have they drugged you or hypnotized you or something?"

She snickered nervously.

"You call me an idiot," she said to Mrs. Never-dead. "This one's your prize idiot. Elmo the idiot."

"Oh, shut up." Mrs. Never-dead waved the crowbar at us, pointing to the door.

Elmo the idiot. Elmo the soon-to-be-dead. Saint Elmo. Saint Elmo's fire. The thoughts spun around in my head, and one stuck. *Saint Elmo's fire . . .*

"Walk," said Mr. Never-dead. "And don't try anything."

They herded us out of the room. We started shuffling down the stairs. I was in front. Mr. Never-dead was beside me; Mrs. Never-dead and Aunt Vivien were behind the others.

The long hallway loomed ahead of me. It was still in darkness.

Saint Elmo's fire . . .

It might not work, but it was worth a try. If we did nothing, we were dead.

I tensed, waiting for my chance.

"Keep moving," shouted Mrs. Never-dead. "And keep your eyes open!" Her husband turned slightly at the sound of her voice.

Now!

I leaped the last four steps and rolled into the darkness of the hallway. I staggered to my feet. . . .

Bang!

The sudden clatter nearly frightened me to death. I had felt the wind in my hair as a spinning lead pipe whizzed past my head. It crashed through the window in front of me. It must have only missed me by an inch.

I heard the Never-deads yelling and swearing as I thundered down the hallway. The rest of the gang had dropped to the ground as the window shattered. The Never-deads were falling over them. *Good, good!*

I reached the heavy, carved door, shot through it, and headed for the kitchen. The door there was still bolted. The Never-deads must have gotten into the house through a window, as Tom had said they would.

I grabbed what I needed, then wrestled the bolt open and flew out the door, slamming it behind me.

Vaguely I noticed that the storm had passed. But the storm inside the house was more violent than ever. I'd heard yells and running feet as I slammed the door.

In a minute, they'd catch up to me. I knew I'd never get away. But if only I had time to do what I planned . . .

I pelted around to the back of the house, my fingers fumbling with what I had in my hand.

It only took a moment. And then I was hurtling back. Back toward the kitchen. I didn't want to run into danger. But I knew I had to if my plan was going to have a chance of working.

Mr. Never-dead came bursting through the kitchen door, dragging Liz behind him. He saw me and grabbed Liz in a chokehold.

"Get back in here or she's dead!" he yelled.

I knew he wasn't bluffing.

"Okay," I said. "Let her go. I'm coming in."

As soon as I got near him, he grabbed me. Then he hurried Liz and me back to the room with the heavy, carved door and the circular table with its twelve chairs.

Mrs. Never-dead, Aunt Vivien, and the others were there. Aunt Vivien was sniffing again and looking nervous.

Mrs. Never-dead was still waving the crowbar at Nick, Tom, and Richelle. They were standing very still.

"Got him," said Mr. Never-dead with satisfaction.

"All right," said his wife. "You did something right for a change. Now we'll take them to the well."

I saw Tom go pale. Richelle clung to Liz's arm, her lips quivering.

Mrs. Never-dead turned to Aunt Vivien. "You stay here and keep watch," she ordered. "We won't be long."

"I'm not staying here on my own. What if . . . ?" quavered Aunt Vivien.

"You brainless ninny!" exploded Mrs. Never-dead. "Something would have happened by now if she was still here. Just do as I say! And stop that disgusting sniffing!"

Something seemed odd. And finally, I realized what it was. The Never-deads and Aunt Vivien seemed even more nervous than we were.

Despite their ferocious anger, they — especially Aunt Vivien — were scared of Sunny. Something had happened to convince them that she was a dangerous enemy.

She is, too. But she looks so small and fragile that not many people realize it. They don't know she's a tae kwon do black belt, and that because of gym, she's got muscles on her muscles.

Mr. and Mrs. Never-dead savagely pushed us out of the room and toward the front door. They were going to take us out that way.

I was wondering whether I should try another risky move. I

was wondering also whether my dash to the backyard had been of any use or not.

Mr. Never-dead reached out to open the front door. . . .

And suddenly there was a muffled yell and a dull thud from the room we'd just left.

The Never-deads hesitated, then looked at one another.

"It's probably nothing," she said. "Go and have a look."

Unwillingly, he began walking back the way we'd come.

Mrs. Never-dead kept her weapon pointed at us. "Don't try anything silly," she warned.

We waited, straining our ears to hear what was happening inside the house. But there wasn't a sound.

Minutes crawled by. But Mr. Never-dead didn't come back.

"Something's happened to him," said Tom, casually.

"Looks like it," nodded Nick.

"Maybe we should go and see," Liz put in.

"Shut up!" spat Mrs. Never-dead. She was sweating. She licked her lips nervously.

We waited. Finally, she could stand it no longer.

"All right!" she snapped. "Go back there. Hands on your heads. And don't forget. I'll be right behind you."

We walked slowly back into the room with the carved door and the big round table. It was empty. There was no sign of either Mr. Never-dead or Aunt Vivien.

"Kevin!" called Mrs. Never-dead. And I was pleased to hear her voice crack. She was worried.

But she still had that crowbar. Holding it in front of her, she looked carefully around the room.

We looked, too. Where was Sunny?

We saw it, a second before she did. Liz's bedroom door was open. It was open just a crack. But it had definitely been closed when we were in this room before.

We knew it, and she knew it.

"I see," she said. "We're playing hide-and-seek."

She waved the crowbar at us, silently telling us to go toward the bedroom. We did what she wanted.

"Go in," she said, with a nasty smile. "One by one. Off you go. I want you all in the same place."

She pushed open the door. The room was completely dark. We filed in. First Liz, then Nick, then Richelle, then Tom. And I was last.

We could see nothing. We stood in the middle of the floor, listening to each other breathing.

"Sunny?" whispered Liz. But there was no answer.

"Now," said Mrs. Never-dead's voice from the doorway, "I'm going to turn on the light. And just remember, I'm armed and dangerous."

The door creaked open. Mrs. Never-dead reached for the light switch and clicked it. But the light didn't come on.

She stepped through the doorway. And then it happened. The most terrifying moment of my life.

"Down!" roared a voice.

And at exactly the same moment, as we were diving for the carpet, the door swung back at Mrs. Never-dead. It crashed into her nose and forehead, knocking her back out of the bedroom. She fell flat on her back in the mezzanine. The crowbar flew upward and landed just beside me with a thud.

At the same time, I rolled to one side and bumped into the body of someone lying by the side of the bed. In the darkness I could see the white of a gag, and white strips binding feet and wrists. But I didn't have any idea who the person was.

Then the body sniffed.

"Aunt Vivien!" I yelled. "Are you all right?"

"Of course I am!"

The light in the bedroom went on.

I blinked in amazement. Aunt Vivien was lying beside me, gagged and tied up like a mummy.

Mr. Never-dead was lying in the other corner of the room in the same state.

Mrs. Never-dead was flat on her back just outside. Sunny was kneeling beside her calmly tying up her wrists with what looked like strips of rag.

And in the center of the bedroom, a fierce-looking old woman had just finished screwing the lightbulb back in its socket.

16

Terror in the dark

I stood there for a minute. Amazed. Dazed. Speechless.

In an instant, I could see who the old woman was.

She was my great-aunt. She was Vivien Zimmer. She looked so much like Grandad. She was tall, and straight, and strong-looking. And tough. Really tough.

"But if this is the real Aunt Vivien," I asked myself, "who's that in the long brown skirt?"

With the room light on, she was a pitiful sight. Black eye, injured forehead, hair damp and tangled. The real Aunt Vivien stepped over to her and took off the gag. Not very gently.

"Don't let her near me. Keep her away," wailed the pathetic creature on the floor.

The real Aunt Vivien looked down scornfully. "I won't hurt you," she said. "I wouldn't waste the energy." Then she looked me up and down.

"You must be Elmo," she said. "I'd know you anywhere, even if I hadn't seen your picture in the *Pen*. You looked exactly the same when you were three months old. Only you had less hair."

The gang looked at me. And I could tell they were thinking: *Elmo, the cute and cuddly thing.* I turned away.

"Why didn't you do what I said in my note?" she demanded. "Then everything would have been so simple! You call yourself a Zimmer?"

"We . . . um . . . did do what it said," I stammered.

"We tried to," nodded Liz.

"No, you didn't!" she snapped. "If you had, you wouldn't be here now."

I pulled the crumpled poster out of my pocket and smoothed it out.

THE KILLER vs. THE FREAK

TWO DEADLY ENEMIES LOCKED IN FIGHT TO THE DEATH.

KNEEBONE TOWN HALL, SATURDAY NIGHT.
BE THERE!

I pointed at the highlighted words, and the signature letter.

TWO DEADLY ENEMIES . . .
FIGHT TO THE DEATH. V.

I read. "Well, we tried to fight. We tried to save you, Aunt Vivien. I know we didn't do terribly well, but . . ."

She gave a huge roar of laughter. "No, you silly boy! That's not the message. Those words aren't highlighted. They're *crossed out!*"

I blinked at the poster. Slowly I read aloud the words that *weren't* marked with blood:

"LOCKED IN . . . KNEEBONE TOWN HALL, SATURDAY NIGHT. BE THERE!"

"Oh!" I heard Richelle say blankly.

"I simply wanted to tell you where I was, and to tell you to go to Kneebone Town Hall tonight to get help," said my extraordinary great-aunt. "Everyone will be there, you know. The town will be crawling with police, in particular. They love the wrestling around here."

I stared at her with my mouth open, my mind spinning with about a million questions.

"I certainly didn't want you running around here risking your lives," she went on, frowning quite crossly. "What would your father say if he knew?"

●

Aunt Vivien locked the Never-deads and the fake Aunt Vivien into the bedroom and took us down to the kitchen.

"Now," she said briskly. "One of you can drive to Kneebone and get the police."

"There isn't a driveable car," said Nick.

She clicked her tongue impatiently.

"Of course there is!" she said. "I told those Everedd idiots the Rolls had shoddy brakes. But of course it doesn't. It's in perfect working order. Or there's the SUV, if you'd prefer. Big green thing. They've probably put it in the garage next to the Rolls."

"A shiny green SUV?" I asked slowly.

She nodded.

"A green SUV passed us on the way here," said Sunny.

"That's right," said Richelle. "The driver was drinking a can of Coke. I could have killed him for it."

"The driver was a man with a ponytail," I said.

I suddenly saw it all. The light had finally dawned.

It was him. The man with the ponytail was the fake Aunt Vivien. He'd been Mrs. Never-dead's solution to the problem of Help-for-Hire turning up at just the wrong moment.

The long hair was real. So the fake Aunt Vivien had fooled us completely. Richelle would have spotted a wig in a second.

"How," said Aunt Vivien severely, "you could ever have thought that ridiculous man was me, I can't imagine."

I bit my lip. "I didn't know what you looked like," I mumbled.

"He brought me some food last night. Still dressed in that horrible get-up she'd made him put on," Aunt Vivien fumed. "I was so mad that as soon as he untied my hands so I could eat, I punched him in the eye."

There was a shout of laughter from the gang.

"We . . . we heard a scream in the night. We saw the black eye the next day. We thought the Never-deads were roughing you up," I stammered. "And all the time it was you doing the damage. I don't believe it!"

"Anyway," said Aunt Vivien. "Take the car —"

"But . . . um . . . none of us can drive," I cut in.

"Do I have to do *everything* myself?" she asked briskly. "I have to stay here. I don't trust those nasty customers upstairs."

While we were thinking about that, we heard a siren. Coming closer.

"Must be a fire somewhere," said Aunt Vivien.

Then I remembered. "Yes!" I yelled. "It worked! Hey, it worked!"

"What worked?" everyone asked.

"Come and see!"

Outside, in the backyard, the pile of junk we'd moved from the garage was burning like mad. It was a huge blaze. The fire I'd lit, in the few seconds I had between running away from the Never-deads and giving myself up again, had really taken hold.

Up the Mistfall driveway roared two fire engines and a police car, sirens blaring.

Elmo's fire. Not as romantic as Saint Elmo's fire, maybe. But more successful as protection.

Just as I'd hoped, the bonfire had drawn more attention to Mistfall than a hundred people going for help.

The police and fire brigade — and I guess everyone for miles around — had been able to see the blaze. It was huge.

"Elmo," said Aunt Vivien, squeezing my shoulder, "you're a smart thinker. You're a real Zimmer, after all."

While the firefighters put out the bonfire, the police came in to see if everything was okay. It turned out they were friends of Aunt Vivien.

"Well, well, well," said the sergeant, when we showed them the three tied-up crooks. "I do believe it's old 'Sniffer' Brindley behind that black eye."

"You know him, George?" asked Aunt Vivien.

"Know him?" he echoed. "He'd qualify for the *Guinness Book of Records* as the stupidest small-time crook this side of the Mississippi. And who are these two? Let's have a look at them."

Mr. and Mrs. Never-dead stood silently with their heads down. Aunt Vivien took one head in each hand and jerked them up for the sergeant to see.

"Ha! I might have known," he said. "The Everedds. Brother and sister. Got a record as long as my arm, and wanted in a couple of states, to boot."

He told the two officers with him to take the Everedds away.

"Viv," he said to my great-aunt, after they'd gone, "get a phone line installed, will you? You can't go lighting fires every time you want to call the cops."

Heavy footsteps pounded the floorboards in the hall. I guess I was still very nervous. *Lucky the police are still in the house*, I thought.

It was the two big guys from the train. A little guy was with them.

"We were on our way to Kneebone when we saw the fire," one of the big guys said.

"Yeah," said the other. "Thought you might need some help. What happened?"

The sergeant explained and thanked them for stopping.

"Hey," said one of the big guys. "Aren't you the kids who came up on the same train as us?"

We nodded.

"Well, don't let a little thing like this spoil your weekend." He turned to the little guy. "Got any tickets?"

The little guy put his hand in the inside pocket of his coat.

"Got a few spare ones, Bill," he said.

"How'd ya like to come to the wrestling match?" said Bill.

"I'd *love* to," said Aunt Vivien, before any of the rest of us had a chance to say anything.

"You're on!" grinned Bill. "Jumbo and I are on tonight at Kneebone town hall. Y'know? The Killer and The Freak?"

I couldn't believe it. These guys were deadly *enemies*? They seemed like the best of friends.

"Aren't you supposed to fight to the death?" asked Richelle, staring at them.

The wrestlers laughed.

"That's right," Bill said. "We always fight to the death, don't we, Jumbo?"

"Yeah. That's right," said Jumbo. "Sometimes he dies. Sometimes I die. Ask our manager."

They roared with laughter and slapped each other on the back. Bill, their manager, just nodded and laughed with them.

"See you later," Frank said.

"Yeah," Bill said. "It's his turn to die tonight."

They were still laughing as they got into the big black car and drove away.

17

Answers

We sat around the kitchen table after everyone had gone. Aunt Vivien raided the fridge and pantry and plunked everything down. Ham, tomatoes, potato salad, chicken, ice cream, cakes, drinks, potato chips — everything she could lay her hands on.

It was a feast. And for a while, we did nothing but eat.

Then Aunt Vivien reached over and patted Sunny's hand.

"You've got a useful friend here," she said. "She's very quick on her feet. Sniffer nabbed her, trying to slip out."

Sunny made a face. She wasn't very proud of being caught. "The Never-deads were in the kitchen. I thought they were the only ones I had to watch out for," she said. "I was just getting through a back window, when he grabbed me."

Aunt Vivien took up the story. "Anyway, he tied her up and dumped her in the tower room, with me. Then he ran off to tell the Everedds."

She smiled with remembered pleasure, and took a spoonful of chocolate ice cream.

"By the time he came back to check on us, after the lights went out, we were ready for him. We'd untied each other. We tackled him as he came through the door. Knocked him out. Then we tied him up and left him there. Oh, Sunny was a brave little soldier."

Sunny isn't good at being praised. She didn't say anything.

"We holed up. We were going to wait for our chance to pick off the Never-deads, as you call them, one by one," Aunt Vivien went on. "We couldn't take any risks. I knew they had weapons. That's how they caught me in the first place."

Sunny grinned. "But then everything got complicated," she said. "People running around. Odd noises. Then they had you as hostages. We had to be very careful. So we stayed hidden till the time was right. Vivien worked it all out."

I could see by the look on her face that she thought my Aunt Vivien was a pretty brave soldier, too.

But we all wanted to know more. In fact, I for one had about a thousand questions to ask. I settled for the most important one.

"Why did the Everedds come here?" I asked.

Aunt Vivien held her head up. Her lined face was proud, and her eyes were bright and sharp. I'd seen the same expression on Grandad's face.

Like she said — how could I have thought for a second that Sniffer Brindley was the real Vivien Zimmer?

"Elmo, you heard about me from your grandfather, didn't you?" she asked.

I nodded and felt myself blushing. She smiled.

"You've heard how silly and selfish I am, and how I've traveled around the world all my life, just living it up?" she persisted.

"Um — sort of," I mumbled.

"Well," said Aunt Vivien cheerfully, "that's what everyone

thought. I'm retired now. So there's no harm telling you, though I'd ask you to keep it under your hats. Up until a few years ago, I was what you might call a secret agent."

"Wow," said Tom. "You mean a spy?"

She grinned at him. "In a way. Mostly it was pretty ordinary stuff. Passing messages. Delivering packages. Microfilm. That sort of stuff."

"Weren't you worried about getting caught?" asked Richelle. "Spies often get caught in the movies."

"They often did, and still do, in real life," Aunt Vivien said. "It's a risk one has to take. But if you worry about getting caught, you might as well give it up."

She grinned again. "But I was lucky. No one suspected me. Not even my brother, Elmo's grandfather. He was always terribly snobby about my traveling. Thought I should have settled down and raised a family, like he did. But that wasn't my style. And, of course, I couldn't tell him what I was really doing."

I could hardly believe what I was hearing. But I knew I had to. "So, if you've retired now, why did the Everedds take you prisoner, Aunt Vivien?" I asked.

She shrugged. "Because they're incredibly stupid people," she said.

We stared at her. Tom helped himself to more ham, and a chicken leg to go with it.

"Stories make me hungry," he explained, when Liz frowned at him.

"It was like this," said Aunt Vivien. "A few months ago, a very dear friend from the old days was in this country, and he came to see me. Sniffer Brindley — one of the local bad apples, as you must have gathered — overheard a conversation I had with this friend. We were in the Kneebone Diner, remembering the old days.

"We talked about a huge stash of gold bars we'd once been involved with. Many, many years ago, after World War II."

She smiled, her eyes full of memories. "I won't tell you the details," she went on. "Enough to say that the gold was in a safe in a Swiss bank. My friend had one key. I had the other. The safe could only be opened by using both keys together. My friend had brought his key with him. And that night in the hotel he gave it to me, as a keepsake."

Liz's eyes were dreamy with romance. But I could see that Nick was on the edge of his chair. I knew what he wanted to know. I wanted to know it, too.

"And do you still have your key, Aunt Vivien?" I asked.

"That's what the Everedds were after," she said. "Sniffer Brindley was somehow connected with them, and he told them what he'd heard and seen in the hotel. So they came here and held me prisoner. They wanted to go and get the gold, you see."

She grinned, and for a moment, she looked very young. "I had my friend's key. But the truth is, I don't know where my own key is. I really don't. I know I put it away somewhere safe, but I've completely forgotten where. I couldn't have told the Everedds where it was to save my life."

I dug into my jeans pocket and pulled out the key that had been tied to the little box Richelle found in the Rolls.

"Is this it?" I asked, and told her where we'd found it.

She stared at it. "You know, I think it is," she said slowly, turning it over in her hand.

"That means you can go to Switzerland and get the gold," Nick said. I'd swear that he was already deciding how to spend his share.

Aunt Vivien laughed a very hearty laugh.

"Oh, if only," she said. "But after the war, the Swiss bank released it to the proper government of the country concerned, without worrying about the keys. There hasn't been any gold in that safe for ages!"

"Why didn't you tell the Everedds that?" Liz asked.

"I did, Liz. Over and over. Till I was sick of the sound of my own voice. But they thought I was lying."

"They *were* pretty stupid, then, weren't they?" said Nick. He was handling his disappointment well, I thought.

"Stupid!" Aunt Vivien exclaimed. "Stupid isn't the word for it. But anyway, they're out of the way now. And I suggest we change our clothes, and go watch some wrestling now."

"In the *Rolls*?" exclaimed Richelle, clasping her hands with delight.

"Certainly," said Aunt Vivien, licking the last of the chocolate ice cream from her lips. "How else?"

On Sunday, we had a huge lunch. The wrestlers, the police sergeant, and some other friends of Aunt Vivien's joined us. It was a great party. And we loved every minute of it.

When it was time to leave for the train on Monday, Aunt Vivien paid us three times what we would have been paid if we'd worked the entire time we were there.

We looked at each other. Liz spoke for us all.

"We can't take it," she said. "We haven't worked for it. Well, not for as much as that."

"Don't be ridiculous," cried Aunt Vivien. "Haven't you heard of hazard pay? I insist that you take it."

So we did. As Nick said, who's going to argue with a woman like Aunt Vivien?

At the station, Aunt Vivien gave everyone in the gang a big hug and thanked them.

Then she hugged me. "It's good to know you at last, Elmo," she said. "In your own way, you're as handy as Sunny. You're a real thinker. Lighting that fire was a stroke of genius. Come and see me again. Will you?"

"Of course I will," I said.

She gave me another hug.

"Give my regards to your father. You can tell him about me if you like. Then he might understand why I've kept away from the family all these years."

Just as the train was starting, I put my head out the window and asked her one last question.

"If you'd known where the other key was, and if the gold was still in the vault, would you have told the Never-deads?"

She looked at me scornfully.

"Of course not, you silly boy. Would you?"

I didn't answer. The train pulled away from the station.

"No, of course you wouldn't," she called after it, waving. "You're a real Zimmer, Saint Elmo."

And that thought kept me happy all the long way home.

Want to know what happens next?
Here's a sneak peek from:

**EMILY RODDA'S
RAVEN HILL MYSTERIES**

CASE #5: DIRTY TRICKS

EMILY RODDA'S
RAVEN HILL MYSTERIES

CASE #5: DIRTY TRICKS

It all started at Raven Hill High — in class, one cold, rainy, wintry Monday morning. Our new student English teacher, Mr. Raven, was giving us an assignment. As if a rainy Monday morning wasn't back luck enough.

Mr. Raven was weird. He wore a dark suit and black-framed rectangular glasses. He was very thin and pale, and he had straight, shoulder-length black hair and big, pale green eyes.

He didn't look like your average student teacher, in other words. He didn't seem to have that awful, bright enthusiasm that most student teachers have, either. His voice was soft and low and never changed tone at all. It never went up, and it never went down.

In fact, there was something quite spooky about him. A few of the guys at the back of the class had tried to give him a hard time early in the lesson. But he'd just kind of looked at them with those pale green eyes and they shut up.

He handed out photocopied sheets to everyone. I looked at my copy. It was headed "Alphabetical Mysteries." Underneath was a list of words in alphabetical order: *Alphabet, Bees, Chameleon, Doughnut,* and so on, all the way down to *Zodiac.*

Mr. Raven told us that, as there were twenty-six of us in the class, and twenty-six letters in the alphabet, there was one topic on the list for each of us.

"A most fortunate coincidence," he said softly, pushing his hair behind his ears with long, bony fingers. "I am very fond of the alphabet." His thin lips curved in what I guess was a smile. It was a weird, curvy smile that didn't show his teeth.

I looked at Liz and Nick, who were sitting on my left. We've been stuck with some weird teachers before, but it looked like Mr. Raven was going to be the worst yet. Nick rolled his eyes back at me, and Liz covered a smile with her hand.

"You are each to choose one of these topics, and research it at Raven Hill Library," Mr. Raven went on. "It's very important to develop good library skills. It is also good to support your local library by using it regularly."

"And by paying library fines," groaned Tom on my right, as he sketched cartoons of Mr. Raven all over his list of topics. I pretended I hadn't heard him. For days we'd been hearing about Tom's lost library book, and getting updates of everywhere he'd looked for it. I never listened when he got started. If only he'd be a bit more organized he wouldn't get himself into these messes.

"As I told you all when I introduced myself," continued Mr. Raven, perching carefully on the edge of his desk, "until a few weeks ago I worked part-time at Raven Hill Library. So I know that they have books on all these topics."

I gazed at the clock helplessly and listened to the rain beating down outside. I hate assignments. And these topics were really weird. E for Elephant. F for Fingerprint. G for Gypsy. Apart from the fact that they were all in a list together, they seemed to have nothing in common.

Fortunately, I wasn't the only one who was confused.

"These topics are all very different from one another, Mr. Raven," said Sunny's flat, practical voice from the row in front of me. "I don't really understand what we have to do."

Mr. Raven gave that strange little smile again and sat up straighter on the edge of his desk.

"The assignment title is the clue," he said. "'Alphabetical Mysteries.' You'll find that every one of the topics on this list involves some kind of mystery."

A flash of lightning lit up the room and I jumped. He paused until the thunder crashed a second or two later, and a shiver ran up and down my spine. He didn't have to be so dark and spooky in the middle of a storm! Not when there were people as sensitive as me in the class. I get spooked really easily.

"Mystery?" said Elmo, who was sitting next to Sunny. I could see him leaning forward on his desk. I could just imagine his eyes sparkling. Trust Elmo to be interested.

Mr. Raven nodded. "There is something about each of these topics that is not widely known, or not fully understood, or is just surprising or unusual," he said.

"So how come P is for Phobia instead of Phantom?" some idiot called out from the back. Bradley Henshaw, probably.

Everyone snickered. Thanks to our local paper, the *Pen*, everyone knew about the so-called Phantom of the Library, and the tricks he had been playing for the last month. Everyone thought they were so funny. Everyone but me, that is.

Mr. Raven ignored the interruption. "I have my own ideas," he went on. "But it's up to each of you to choose your topic and then discover and describe the mystery that *you* see within it."

It sounded pretty boring to me. I looked at the list again. I couldn't see anything mysterious about most of these topics. Elephants? Elephants are elephants. Doughnut? What's mysterious about a doughnut? It's fattening. It's round. That's all.

"When's it due?" asked Nick, getting down to basics.

"Next Monday," answered Mr. Raven briefly.

Just a week! There was a bit of complaining about that, but he raised his hand for silence. "The research won't take long," he said calmly. "Then you need only write as much as you need to explain the mystery. And give a list of the books you've used to discover it."

I wriggled uncomfortably on my chair.

"I suggest you waste no time in choosing your topic," said Mr. Raven as the bell rang. I sprang to my feet in relief. I couldn't wait to get out of there.

To my surprise, most of the other kids crowded around Mr. Raven's desk, trying to get in first with their choices. Some of them seemed really excited.

"X! X! I want X!" I heard Tom yell. I checked my sheet. X-ray.

"X-ray. Of course. It couldn't be anything else. Except Xylophone, I suppose," I said gloomily.

"What about Xylem? Or Xenophobia?" asked Elmo.

I nodded to make it seem like I knew what those words

meant, and left without putting my name down for anything. The thunder rumbled loudly, like a warning that trouble lay ahead.

I should have listened to it.

To be continued . . .

WHO'S BEHIND T
PRANKS IN THE LIBI

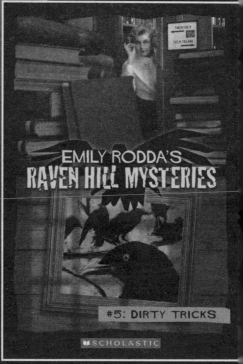

EMILY RODDA'S
RAVEN HILL MYSTERIES

#5: DIRTY TRICKS

■SCHOLASTIC

The Help-for-Hire gang has too much homework!
library seems like a great place to hit the books—
books start hitting back. The Phantom of the Libra
practical jokes. But as the tricks turn more treache
Richelle races to unmask the Phantom.

Welcome to Raven Hill. . .where danger mea

■SCHOLASTIC